The Rupa Bo

SHIKAR STORIES

Other Ruskin Bond Titles

The Rupa Book of
SHIKAR STORIES

Edited by
Ruskin Bond

Rupa & Co

Published by

Rupa & Co

7/16, Ansari Road, Daryaganj,
New Delhi 110 002

Sales Centres:

Allahabad Bangalooru Chandigarh Chennai
Hyderabad Jaipur Kathmandu
Kolkata Mumbai Pune

Typeset in 11 pts. Revival by
Nikita Overseas Pvt. Ltd.
1410 Chiranjiv Tower
43 Nehru Place
New Delhi 110 019

Printed in India by
Rekha Printers Pvt. Ltd.
A-102/1 Okhla Industrial Area, Phase-II
New Delhi-110 020

Contents

Introduction

Some hunted for sport, others for commercial reasons. Some hunted for self-protection, or to rid an area of a dreaded man-eater or cattle-lifter.

Sixty and more years ago, the forests were extensive, wildlife abundant. Hunting was the sport of kings, officers and gentlemen. You were pretty low on the social scale if you had not bagged a couple of tigers. Big-game hunters, amateur shikaris, surveyors, administrators, all had their own thrilling experiences to relate, and many of these factual accounts appeared in the magazines of the 1920s and 1930s, a period when the popularity of "shikar" was at its peak. Some wrote under their own names. Others used pseudonyms, possibly to hide the fact that they had been spending a great deal of time away from their official duties! With one exception, none of these stories has appeared before between book covers. They have been selected from my collection of *Indian State Railways magazines* of that period.

It was a period when the walls of almost every official or civilian residence were adorned with the mounted heads of tiger and panther, or the antlers of chital, sambhur or antelope. But not everyone who entered the jungle went in with guns blazing

F.W. Champion of the Indian Forest Service, was a pioneering wildlife photographer who preferred to do his shooting with a camera. His books, *With A Camera in Tigerland* and *The Jungle in Sunlight and Shadow*, reveal a knowledge of the jungle, wild-life and natural history equal to that of Jim Corbett or Kenneth Anderson.

Indeed, most of the writers represented in this collection—C.H. Donald, C.A. Kincaid, Augustus Somerville, C.H. Dawson—acquired an intimate knowledge of the jungle and its ways: Somerville, in his wanderings as a Surveyor; Kincaid as a curious and well-read Civil Servant who served in many parts of the country; Donald, who spent many years in the hills around Simla; 'Nimrod', who loved the Narmada....

About five years ago, when I was taking an elephant ride through the forest of the Rajaji Sanctuary near Hardwar, the elderly mahout who was my guide told me that he had been Champion's mahout when he was just a boy. He showed me plenty of wild boar, cheetal and sambhur, but alas, there were no longer any tigers in the area; they had all gone, shot into extinction in the 1950s, when the Indian nouveau-riche plundered the forests of what little the British had left behind. It was really the coming of the jeep that helped finish off the larger carnivores. No longer dependent on elephants or beaters, shikaris could drive along the narrow forest roads, and many used powerful headlights or searchlights to render these animals helpless targets.

As a boy, I had the mortification of being on some of these expeditions, my stepfather being an inveterate poacher. But on one occasion the hunters were hunted. Their jeep backed into a nest of vicious red ants. In a twinkling the shikaris were covered with the brutes, all intent on finding the softest portions of the human anatomy, biting with vicious little nips. The expedition beat a hasty retreat.

Another creature that is more than a match for humans is the big bee, common throughout the country. When disturbed it will attack both man and beast with the utmost fierceness.

There are many stories about the big bee and its vindictive ways. Two shikaris were resting between beats one hot May morning in the jungle. One of them unwarily lit a pipe. Overhead spread the crown of a talk silk-cotton tree with a dozen great combs of the big bee attached to its branches. Resenting the intrusion and the pipe smoke, the bees lost no time in launching an offensive.

It was an utter rout, and the elder of the two shikaris, a respected bald-headed Colonel of H.M.'s Regiments of Foot, led the retreat, which was lacking in both dignity and strategy. They fled towards the open country, and when the bees finally left them, the Colonel had to all appearances suddenly grown a stiff crop of bristles all over his pate. It took a lot of attention, profane language, and soothing ointments to get rid of all those bee-stings.

The Animal Kingdom is made up largely of two great groups of animals, the predators and the preyed upon. This also holds good for the insect world. In the words of the old jingle—

> Greater bugs eat lesser bugs,
> And so on, *ad infinitum.*

There was a time when tigers were prevalent throughout the country, and the depredations of man-eaters and cattle-lifters did justify the hunting of these predators. But motives were often mixed, and hunting as a sport usually took precedence over hunting for the protection of villages and their livestock.

What is clear from the writings of these shikari-sportsmen is that many of them grew to love the jungle—camp life, the great outdoors, the richness of flora and fauna. From being hunters, a few became naturalists. And, once the jungle wove its spell, these men would return to it again and again. Not for gain, as is the case today; but for the feeling of freedom that only the jungle could give them.

"The pleasure of shikar is not all in successful results," wrote 'Nimrod'. "The joy of living the jungle life; the peace, and the being so close to nature, is the greater part of sport. And so, though without trophies, we are content and strike our camp, to proceed to other jungle resorts without any regrets in our minds."

This represented the attitude and outlook of the finer type of sportsman.

Ruskin Bond
Landour, Mussoorie

The Tiger and the Terrier

By Brig.-General R.G. Burton

There was a time when "griffins", as newcomers used to be called, expected to find tigers in their gardens and snakes in their boots when they went to India; but even thirty years ago such ideas were no longer prevalent, and were supposed to be found only in the tales of those eminent Anglo-Indians, Colonels Monsoon and Bowlong. But I was no novice when I arrived at a military cantonment in the Deccan in November 1898 and observed what a "jungly" appearance it presented. Indeed, my first walk induced me to remark to my companion on the tigerish look of a nullah which ran through the place and was at that time overgrown with the luxuriant foliage of the rainy season.

But there were, so far as we knew, no tigers within a radius of fifty or sixty miles, and no jungles to hold them, although a tomb in the old cemetery recorded that an officer had been killed by one of these animals ten miles off about seventy years before this time. A tiger requires extensive jungles for its wanderings, and the country around us was now mostly under cultivation with some sparse bush and wasteland on the hills. Yet, even then, all unknown to us, a tiger was padding his way towards the cantonment, and he had been seen, as I learnt long afterwards, by an old friend, a Muhammadan Mullah who was waiting in ambush for more harmless animals near a pool and whose heart "turned to water" as he expressed it, at the sight of a monster such as he had never seen before. Leopards he was familiar with, for they were plentiful in his district twenty miles away, but the greatest cat of all was strange to him.

Adjoining the large compound in which my house stood was a garden some acres in extent containing a bungalow now empty, the dwelling place of a missionary who for many years did excellent and devoted work in the surrounding country. Here, in his absence a gardener was employed to keep the place in order. Only a day or two after my arrival from leave in England, the gardener came over to say that he had seen what he described as a leopard lying down in the verandah of the unoccupied bungalow. Such simple people are prone to exaggeration, and it was thought more probable that the animal was a wild or a large domestic cat. However, with a few followers and two sepoys we two turned out with our rifles, only to find the verandah empty. The gardener was, however, so sure that we decided to beat through an extensive patch of long grass in the compound, into which the animal must have retreated.

The two guns took up a position on the farther side of this patch while the men walked in line towards them. Suddenly, there was a rush and a roar, and not a leopard but a well-grown tiger, whose voice was at once recognisable, broke from the cover and sprang over the hedge, disappearing in a moment without giving the guns time to fire a shot. The tiger had made off as soon as it was disturbed, but in passing found time to strike down one of the sepoys and inflict some severe wounds on his back and shoulder. He was taken to hospital and made a good recovery in the course of a few weeks, although not in time to accompany us on the annual tiger-hunting expedition. No doubt, he had enough of tigers to last him the remainder of this life!

We then followed the tiger, which had disappeared in an adjoining compound. More "guns" had arrived and we walked across the open accompanied by Sal, the bull-terrier, who soon turned the tiger out of a shallow nullah that ran along the hedge on one side of the compound. The animal fled, followed closely by the gallant Sal and by several bullets, fired to the danger of spectators in the vicinity. It was already growing dusk. The tiger had taken refuge in a deep and dense hedge, from which we tried in vain to dislodge it and in which it could not be seen. Darkness came on with the usual rapidity and suddenness. With the aid of lanterns we attempted to make out the lurking animal, but although we went up close and peered into the hedge, nothing could be seen. It was a situation not without danger, especially as the beast had probably been wounded and was certainly angry.

There was nothing to be done but to leave it until morning, when the tracks were taken up where they crossed the dusty road, one halting footmark showing that the tiger was going lame, as indicated also by a few drops of blood. It had evidently retreated soon after nightfall, and a mile farther on it had slaked its thirst at a pool in a nullah on the edge of the cantonment. It then made towards the low hills where the velvet-footed beast left no impression on the hard and stony ground. We beat through the surrounding country and day after day I rode many miles round in the direction taken by the tiger, but no trace of it was found until five days later when a man was seized in a field near a village six miles off; he was mortally wounded, his insides being almost torn out of his body. The unfortunate villager was able to speak, and before he died he related that he had been scaring birds in the *Jowari* (millet) when he heard a peculiar noise and on going towards the spot from which it came he was seized by the animal, which rushed out upon him.

We went to the scene of the tragedy which was in a field where the *jowari* grew to a height of six or seven feet. There we found the poor man's staff and cotton cloth, a pool of blood, and the tracks and a strong smell of the wild beast. We followed through the field and beyond, where the tracks were again lost on hard ground in a wide and rocky nullah. Dog Sal, though so keen and brave in the face of the enemy, seemed to have no nose for tracking.

We encamped upon the spot and next day beat through the nullahs in the neighbourhood without results. But the animal had to be killed. The whole country was in a panic, the people afraid to go out to work in the fields, and we feared to hear of more deaths, for the tiger, so far as we could ascertain, had taken no prey, and must be hungry and desperate; it is of such stuff that man-eaters are made. The district in which the animal had been lost sight of was hilly and broken, containing little water. It was obvious that it would have to find water to quench its thirst; even in normal conditions tigers are impatient of thirst, and doubly so when hunted and wounded. A mile or two across the hills we came to a nullah where there were fresh tracks, and we found a pool where the animal had watered; it was evidently lying up in the adjacent jungle.

We took post while Sal and the men beat through the cover, and the tiger soon broke and galloped across an open strip of ground pursued closely by the bull-terrier barking close at his heels. The chase disappeared in a patch of dense bush and after a succession of roars, howls, and barks Sal emerged, torn and bleeding from extensive wounds in the chest. Still the brave dog wanted to go in again and seek out her enemy, and had to be restrained.

Showers of stones and small shot failed to make the tiger move or give evidence of its situation. Night was coming on and we did not wish to leave it to another day which might involve a further prolonged chase and endanger more lives. Three of us, including a famous Indian officer who still resides near the scene of this encounter, crawled into the bush. After a long search we came suddenly upon the tiger which lay facing us, its eyes blazing in the gloom of the jungle, and appearing ready to charge, but a few shots put an end to its existence.

Poor old Sal was fat, heavy, and not very active, or she might have escaped the cruel claws; as it was she lived a fortnight, and eventually died of exhaustion when the wounds were already healing up. She was photographed with her bandages on the day before her death. The tiger was a male, probably between four and five years old and over eight feet in length. It had a wound which had splintered a bone above one of the hind feet, which showed signs of healing, but must have caused much pain and discomfort, no doubt sustained in the first encounter; there was a slight wound in the flank from a bullet fired when it was driven out on this last occasion, and the final shots were in the chest and the centre of the forehead, where the Subadar-Major's bullet had pierced the brain. The dead animal was carried back to the cantonment, where thousands assembled to view the bold beast which had given so much trouble, and which, they said, had come in search of one who had killed so many of its kind.

Mention has been made of snakes, which were exceedingly abundant in this part of the country. A krait one night left its skin on a teapoy at the bedside; Russell's vipers were numerous, and one that lay in the doorway of a bedroom was nearly trodden upon, but was fortunately betrayed by its loud and persistent hissing. So, tigers in gardens and snakes in bungalows are not only to be found in the tales of our old Indian officers, Bowlong and Monsoon, at any rate they were met with thirty years ago.

The cantonment where these episodes took place has been long since abandoned, and the echoes are for ever silent which once resounded with the tramp of horse and foot and the thunder of guns. In those days the line of rail was nearly hundred miles distant. But should any now wish to travel to the scene of these and many other adventures, or to visit the battlefield where the greatest of English generals gained a famous victory, they need not traverse the long and dusty road along which the pony-tongas used to labour in days gone by. For, they can alight from the train within a mile of the spot where the invading tiger lay up on that November day.

(1929)

A Letter from the Jungle

By 'Nimrod'

You have been promised a letter from the jungle and here, at last, I send it to you.

You have probably not forgotten how cold it was during the time that arctic wave spread all over England (and Europe) early in February. Well, we arrived at our Forest Rest House on the 1st of the month, and that night the whole country was sorely stricken by the same cold wave which passed over the whole of India also, and caused great damage to the crops and the foliage of the forest tracts.

We were in the valley of the Tapti river and the cold was intense. The thermometer hung up in the verandah showed the temperature at six in the morning to be 30°Fahrenheit. Not very cold you will say, comparing that with the cold you experienced, but *really* cold to us dwellers in this warmer climate.

Following on that cold wave the forests of the low-lying country were, and still are, a pitiful sight. All was brown, having

---

*   All temperatures are in Fahrenheit

the appearance of having been burnt, where all should, at that time of the year, have been in every beautiful shade of green. Looking down on the valleys from the higher slopes of the hills one could see quite a distinct line marking the high level, as it were, of the cold wave.

We did not stay long at that camp as the tigers I wanted were absent. They would be there later in the year when the streams and pools in the forests have dried up. Then, the animals would have migrated to the larger streams; for where the animals congregate there will be the tiger and panther which prey upon them.

I went several times along the river looking for tracks, but did not find the sign manual of the Lords of the Forest. It is always very interesting to be out in the early morning at the time when, as the native of the country expresses it, "you can just see the hair on your hand against the sky." That is the time to *see* animals, and birds, too. All the feathered world is busy at the daily task of finding food; and the animals, having been feeding— or on the prowl, according to their nature—all night, are slowly and quietly making their way to secluded places where they can lie up for the day and have undisturbed rest.

The sandy bed of the river shows plainly to our eyes the tracks of all the jungle people who have been abroad during the hours of darkness. Darkness to us but not to them; for not as you imagine it is the darkness of the tropic night. If one does not use an artificial illuminant, one soon becomes accustomed to the light afforded by the stars and finds it sufficient for one's needs. Except when in deep shadow one can see quite well.

But there are certain colours which are not readily visible in twilight and darkness; stare as hard as you wish you will not be able to make out with any distinctness the form of the larger carnivora even at a few yards' distance. It is the ground colour of tawny yellow which is their concealment. Night shooting without the aid of a torch is a very chancy affair.

In the river bed were the tracks of a hyæna, easily distinguishable from those of a panther by the uneven shape of the main pad of the foot; of a porcupine which had come to have a drink; of several wild cats—Great Grandsons of Tom Puss, I call them, of prowling jackals; and of otters. In one place, a long smear in the sand showed where a crocodile had been for a waddling stroll.

Hares love to sport and play in open spaces, and it was evident at one spot that there had been a fine frolic on the part of a couple of these "sons of asses" as natives of some parts of India style them. There were a few tracks of sambur, all hinds and small stags as was plain to the eye; and rounding a bend of the river we saw ahead of us, a couple of hundred yards away, a small stag chital with several hinds. They were re-crossing the river, to gain the security of the Government Forest, after having spent the night among the crops of a village on the further bank.

Peafowl and jungle fowl had been to drink; white egrets were to be seen along the reedy borders of the pools; a pair of Ruddy Sheldrakes—Brahmini ducks of the European sportsman—rose with loud calls of "chakwee, chakwa"; and circling in the sky was a Brahmini kite, a fine handsome bird of bright russet plumage with a conspicuously white head. This bird also is reverenced by Hindus as being sacred to Vishnu, one of their gods.

One day, I went to the higher hills and came across a large sounder of wild pig. Fine animals they were, and no doubt, very excellent pork! But as our servants are Muhammadans, to whom pork in any form is an abomination, the pigs were unmolested. On the way back to camp that day, I passed a place over which I had walked in the morning, and there, over my own tracks, were those of a panther which had no doubt been disturbed by us when we went up the ravine earlier in the day.

After twelve useless days at that camp we moved to another one ten miles south of the river and some six or seven hundred feet higher as to elevation.

The first Rest House was on the very edge of the forest. This one was in a large cultivated clearing into which led six roads, and several paths. Where there are roads and paths, it is much easier to locate the tigers on account of their habit of using these at night during their wanderings in search of game. You can understand that, as it is their business—the business of their very existence—to see and hear and not be seen or heard, it is greatly to their advantage to walk along tracks which allow them to be all eyes and ears without thought of having to tread silent through dry leaves, grass and brushwood.

In order to get tigers, either by beating or by sitting up for them to return to their kill, one has to tie up young buffalo as bait. It sounds cruel but is less cruel than it seems. Death, when it comes to them, is speedy. There is a moment of alarm, it may amount to fright, when they first realise the approach of the feline; and though they may be frightened the first few nights at being left alone in the forest, they soon get used to that, and have but little fear, and no foreknowledge, of what will attack them.

How do I know all that? On very many occasions I have watched all night over live buffaloes and have five times seen what took place when the killing happened. I have also seen panthers kill goats tied up for them and in those cases too the end was merciful.

Sometimes panthers are playful in their killing, like a cat with a mouse, when they see a tethered goat which cannot escape them.

I once saw a panther rush at a goat—these big cats take their prey with a rush, and do not spring upon it—seize it by the neck and run off again! The goat got up, and after a few moments went on with his feed of leaves as if nothing had happened! Perhaps, I may find space in this letter for another incident in illustration of the want of *fear* evidenced by tethered animals; so the old lady who wrote the other day to a writer on shikar, saying he was "a cruel monster and should himself be tethered," was kind-hearted but mistaken.

That camp where all the roads met was a good one for tiger. I shot three there, all stone dead—no, one ran a few yards—so their end was even more merciful than that of their victims.

On the second night of the arrival at the new camp there was a kill on one of the main roads. The tracks in the dust showed that there were two animals at the feast, one a tigress—as could be known by the oval shape of the pug mark—and the other a large male cub. The size of the fang marks in the neck showed that it was the tigress who had done the killing.

I sat up over the kill in a dining room chair, which is quite a comfortable seat for the purpose, and at nine o'clock was made aware of the approach of the pair by a most expressive warning "swear," uttered by the tigress to keep her son from being too hasty to get to his dinner. It was plain to me, and no doubt to him also, that she said "Keep off it you young fool, or you may get it in the neck!"

I was well screened, and sat very quiet. In a few minutes I could see by the light of the moon that a big animal was at the kill, and put up my field glasses. The beast began to feed. The shadows were confusing, but it seemed to be the tigress as the forearm appeared large. I peered and stared, and should have waited for both the animals to be on the kill at the same time.

It was interesting to see the way the tiger used the big claw—the "thumb" of the right paw—to push back the skin and bare the meat of the ribs.

The other animal not showing itself I fired at the shoulder of the feeding beast. To the shot it dashed away into the long grass, but as I heard what seemed to my practised ear a tumble, and no further sound, I knew the tiger must be dead.

At the same time the sound of two or three quiet footsteps came to my ears as the other animals made off and I knew it must be the son, and not the mother, which had been slain.

That this was the case was soon confirmed, as the whole jungle was made aware that the tigress was looking for her son. For the next two hours far and wide she roamed loudly uttering "a-a-ough, a-a-ough" to the terror of the sambur and the four-horned antelope, the barking-deer and the langoors, all of which sounded their alarm calls from time to time. But she did not return to the kill.

In the morning the tiger was found not twenty feet away from the kill. He had been shot through the heart, and in his death rush had turned a complete somersault so that his head was towards where he had come from when fired at. He weighed 180 lbs. and was seven feet long. His paws were large and his forearm as big, almost, as those of his mother. That was what had deceived me, but I ought to have waited. It was a pity I shot him, as he would have grown into a fine tiger.

The next night I again occupied the chair, but had a fruitless vigil. The tigress was around for two hours, calling and bewailing as on the previous evening, but did not come to the kill.

That night a big tiger passed the place where, had I not been sitting up for the tigress, a buffalo would have been tethered. A pity one cannot be in two places at the same time!

The next night, the tigress returned to the kill and had a big feed of very high meat. Had the tree been suitable for a full length machan I would have been in waiting. I decided to give the kill to the vultures and sit up over a live buffalo, as the tigress would be likely to remain in the vicinity.

The moon was now nearly at the full and the night almost as bright as the day. The buffalo—a calf of two years—had a good feed of grass, and then lay down to chew the cud and doubtless, bemoan the hardness of his lot.

It was exactly ten o'clock when I heard him get up. Looking, I saw him staring towards the jungle to my right. Next moment I heard the footsteps of the tigress in the leaves. Until then she had made no sound, but now, knowing herself to be within certain rushing distance of her prey and that it could not escape her, gave up all concealment.

Putting up the field glasses I saw the head of the great brute come into the field of view; then came her long massive form, advancing with slow steps, every muscle ready for instant action and grim purpose in her whole attitude. The fine ruff she wore glistened brightly in the brilliant rays of the moon.

The buffalo remained motionless, staring at the apparition, but when the tigress was about fifteen feet distant he began to struggle to get free. That movement launched the dread beast at him.

I could have killed the tigress as she advanced on the buffalo, but wanted to see the whole affair. And, it was possible that she would have dashed away on the torch shining in her face, for she was an old and cunning beast. The buffalo had to die.

Instantly the killing was over and she appeared to be all on the alert. Then, without further delay, she seized the carcase to drag it away; but finding she could not do this, at once began to break open the hinder parts and commenced her gruesome meal of the still warm and quivering flesh. Nothing to shudder at! Only the same thing, on a larger scale, that your house cat does on most nights of his life.

Interested in all these happenings I delayed my shot overlong, for the beast ceased feeding all of a sudden and went straight off into the forest. She made no attempt to be quiet but went away barking through the jungle as if intoxicated with success, as no doubt she was. All sorts of noises did she make; belchings, zoo noises, queer throaty sounds. The whole forest was aware of her success, and I heard her go further and further away. The animals of the forest seemed to take no notice of her now, as there were no alarm calls; perhaps there were no animals in such an unhealthy neighbourhood, as there had been no announcements of her presence before the killing took place.

It was five hours before she returned, and that she did without a sound, or any warning from the forest dwellers. Instantly, she lay down at the tail end and recommenced her meal.

It was now three in the morning and there could be no further delay. To the light of the torch in her face she looked up. Her eyes shone like balls of emerald. The next instant she lay dead, a p.470 bullet in her neck behind the ears. Her life left her with a great sigh the sound of which came distinctly to my ears as the reverberations of the report of the heavy rifle died away in the stillness of the night.

She measured eight feet three inches between pegs, and weighed 280 lbs. Merciful was her end.

A few days later, a male tiger came past that place and had sun-grilled bones for supper. I sat up for him over a live buffalo but, although he was making zoo noises all around, he did not put in an appearance.

Then, a tigress passed a buffalo, tethered in a river bed, within a few yards, and failed to see it. It had to be tied a few yards—ten, perhaps it was—to one side of the path, but quite in the open. It is not unusual for tigers to miss tethered baits in this way, and such happenings are a strong argument against their having any power of winding their prey. On one occasion, two panthers passed a goat tethered in the open sand in the bed of the Narbada river and failed to see it. Their tracks were within twenty feet!

There followed some days of waiting, but I knew there would be a kill by the big male tiger mentioned above as it is the fixed habit of these felines to cover the same ground about every ten days. On the night of the first of March the expected kill took place. The kill was dragged a matter of five hundred yards, as the root to which the buffalo had been tethered gave way. Yet, it had looked sufficiently strong. Fortunately a suitable tree for the chair was near by, and by four o'clock I was quietly seated.

Beyond the heavy foot fall in the leaves there was no announcement by the jungle folk of the tiger's impending arrival. Just a few minutes earlier and there would have been a daylight shot. He did not pay any attention to the torch, or to the light arranged exactly over the kill to show, before the turning on of the torch, how he was lying, for the night was dark and the kill in deep shadow. He died as he lay, the back of his skull broken to pieces.

This shooting with the aid of a torch is a deadly business, and in course of time—and that not far distant—will have to be prohibited in many forests, or there will be no tigers left. Night shooting of this kind requires much endurance and also intimate knowledge of the habits of these great felines, besides much technique in the matter of numerous details. Fewer animals are wounded than is the case when beating—which is, of course, the more pleasurable method—and there is no risk to the unarmed villager without whose assistance one could obtain no shikar at all. But it *is* a form of shikar of which one gets tired. However, with a slender purse, and such indifferent beaters as the Korkus of the present day who have lost all their jungle instincts and are fast leaving the forests for the open country, the sitting up method is forced upon a large number of sportsmen.

(1929)

A Further Letter from the Jungle

By 'Nimrod'

Our next shooting block was thirty miles south of the one in which I shot those three tigers of which I have given you the history. We sent on our camp kit early in the morning in the small bullock carts of this part of the country, and ourselves went in the car to a Rest House about ten miles along the road. Early the next morning we completed the short distance remaining, and found the carts arrived and our servants settling into the new residence.

Now, I have brought my news up to date and will be able, more or less, to tell you of things as they occur.

All the forests of this part of the country are of teak and bamboo, and the lie of the valleys between the hills is mostly east and west. The average elevation of the main streams is about 1,600 feet above sea level, the adjacent hills being some three or four hundred feet higher, while those to the south of our present camp gradually extend by successive ridges and valleys to the main backbone of the Gawilgarh Hills, the highest point of which is over 3,500 feet in height.

It is now the 9th of April and the hot season is approaching as it is noticeably warmer than it has been, the temperature in the verandah rising to 100deg. in the middle of the day. But the nights are cool, the temperature falling rapidly after sundown. In the early morning it is as low as 56deg.

We are in the valley of a fair sized stream and, as in the Tapti valley so is the case here, all the trees being withered by the frost to a distinctly marked level. Some of the trees are recovering and putting out new leaves, while a few of the more hardy varieties are clothed in the brilliant green of their spring barb, thus giving to the forest the touch of colour needed to relieve the general sameness of the scenery.

As a rule there is not much colour in the forests of tropical countries; there are endless shades of green and brown and, at this season, autumn tints of every description. A few trees there are which gladden our eyes with splashes of colour. One of these—the 'ganiar' of the people—is a tree with a straight trunk which has large handsome saucer-shaped flowers of a bright yellow colour at the ends of the branches. These trees are now leafless, but their new foliage will appear in May. Another tree, also leafless at this time, has brilliant red flowers which are very conspicuous in the forest; it is a species of *erythrina*. Then, there is the well-known tree, called by Europeans 'The Flame of the Forest' on account of the brilliant colour of its velvet-like orange-red petals. Where these trees are plentiful the display of colour is a wonderful sight.

On arrival here we were greeted with the news that there are seven tigers in the vicinity. I was also informed that the news of the countryside is that I have recently shot eight tigers. I fear the story of the seven is as inaccurate as that of the eight, for in walks abroad there is no sign of even one of the reputed seven. A bad sign at this camp is the silence at night. There are no alarm calls of sambur and other animals and no tracks of tiger, old or new. Panthers appear to be absent also.

Yesterday—we have been here ten days now—news came from a village five miles away that a panther had killed a calf the previous afternoon. I went to the place and tracked up the kill, which was very neatly 'butchered' and placed in a clump of bamboos. There was a suitable tree close by and my machan chair soon in position. By five o'clock all was quiet, and the panther could be nowhere in the vicinity. I had every hope of his putting in an appearance at dusk, or soon after, but he did not turn up.

Shortly before dark a lovely mongoose came and had a feed. He was bigger than usual and such a lithe, graceful animal with grey points to the hair of his sleek body and a fine black tip to his long tail. He reminded me of the several of his species which have been such interesting pets from time to time. No snakes, and no cockroaches, or spiders and such like, in one's house when there is a tame mongoose on the premises!

I came away at 9 o'clock and got back to camp and a midnight dinner.

We have a fine pool in the river not far from this bungalow, it is shaded by large trees and has much life about it, and in it. There are many kinds of birds, and almost daily we see the otters at play and the catching of fish. Others besides the otters like a fish diet. On any bare rock in the stream there are cormorants, and at one time or another I have seen four varieties of kingfisher there. One of these is so like the bird one sees in England that you could not tell the difference at sight. Perhaps, there is no difference. One of the others is a black and white bird about twice the size of the little one. His habit is to hover over the water about thirty feet up, plunge deep into the stream, and catch the minnows crosswise in his beak. A poet has described him as 'the pied fish-tiger o'er the pool', a very good description.

The two other kingfishers are alike in colouring, but different in size. Both have bright red bills, and their general appearance is blue and white, mostly blue. The smaller of these is half as big again as the 'fish tiger', while the larger one is more than twice as big again. Also, he is more rare, and only found in heavily wooded country.

Every night, four buffaloes have been tied up at carefully selected places. One night, a panther passed one of the baits but did not touch it. That often happens in these forests. Fourteen days and no kill! But there is likely to be one, as this morning I saw the tracks of a big male tiger along one of the forest cart roads.

It is three days since I wrote as above and I am still tigerless. The night after I saw the tracks, the tiger killed the bait in the river bed to the west of camp. The machan chair was already in position so there was a minimum of disturbance at the place. Owing to the very thick cover, and likelihood of there being no suitable tree near the kill if the tiger was permitted to drag it, the buffalo had been picketted with a wire rope.

An all-night vigil had no result, but in the morning the tracks of the tiger were found in the river bed not far away. I feared that I had come across one of the many very cunning animals of these parts; but sat up the whole of the next night also. Then, it was evident the tiger did not intend to return to the kill and it was made over to the vultures.

Time was running short so I decided to tie up at a place five miles down stream where I found tracks of this same tiger and learnt that his regular haunt was there, in thick cover, between the confluence of two rivers. Owing to the nature of the country a beat would not be likely to succeed so a machan chair was put up and a buffalo tethered on the tiger's tracks.

That was on the night of the 29th. What a pity I did not sit up over the live buffalo! That night he killed it and, a most unusual thing, broke the wire rope. He had unfortunately found the root of a shrub to give him the exact purchase required and was so able to exert the whole of his immense strength. The marks of his fore paws were plain to see.

I tracked up the drag of the kill and found it over a quarter of a mile away, well concealed under a mass of creepers. The tiger had fed at three places during the drag and eaten a great deal.

There was fortunately a suitable tree handy for the machan chair; but it was unfortunately necessary to cut away much of the creepers in order to be able to see. All was quiet at half past four, and at half past seven when it was quite dark, I heard the well-known heavy tread among the leaves, a hundred yards behind me. The nights are very still and one can hear the slightest sound at that distance.

The tiger was extremely cautious, stopping and listening and slowly coming nearer. No doubt, he sat down now and again, as he took nearly an hour to approach close enough to make up his mind that all was clear. Then I heard the quicker steps of the final direct approach and was full of confident expectation. Alas! it was not to be. Having come close enough to see the kill he was able to see that it was not as fully concealed as he had left it. For a tiger of his experience that was sufficient warning. He had no doubt, had a very convincing lesson on some previous occasion and had no intention of taking any risks. Of the watcher in the tree he had, I am sure, no knowledge by any of his senses.

I heard his retreating footsteps and that was the last of him for that night.

In the morning it was found that he had revisited the scene of his kill and removed a shin bone which he had left there.

My permit for this block would be up soon, so I decided that my only sure way of bringing this cunning beast to bag would be to put up the big machan and sleep in it every night until he came along again, as he was sure to do. So, the night of the 31st saw me duly ensconced in a large tree and well screened in.

Every afternoon at three o'clock I set off in a bullock cart, as it was too hot to walk with any pleasure, ate my dinner near the tree and was in the machan and settled down by half an hour before sunset. In the morning I would have a welcome cup of tea from a thermos flask and then walk the five miles back to camp.

I am writing all this in the past tense as I have been disinclined for any writing during these strenuous days!

On the evening of the 5th, I heard the moan of a tiger some way down the river and had hope of the expected kill taking place, but nothing happened. I knew the affair could not now be much delayed as the tiger was bound to be along his former round before long. I was getting tired of the game, but determined to sit him out to the last available moment.

Patience was rewarded on the evening of the 6th—the eighth night's vigil for this beast. At twenty minutes past seven I heard his moaning call down river, same as on the previous evening. Then it came nearer: and at last there was a low call so near that it was certain he must come past me.

There was no sound on the part of any forest animals to announce that the tiger was on the prowl. The buffalo was tethered exactly in the path through the small green bushes of the river bed along which he would come. I lay quietly on my back, listening for any slightest sound, but heard nothing.

At ten minutes to eight there was a rush over the leaf strewn pebbles and a choked bellow on the part of the poor buffalo. In an instant I was sitting up, with rifle out of the loophole and torch shining on the striped hide of the slayer. One very quickly decides where exactly to place the bullet and the foresight gleamed brilliantly on the centre of the shoulder blades as the trigger was pressed.

To the shot the tiger fell on his side exactly as seen in the photographs taken next morning; one from the machan, and the other from the slight elevation of a bullock cart. His tail beat the ground for a few seconds, but there was no other movement. After the tail was quiet, the buffalo's hind legs were kicking, so the tiger breathed his last before his victim ceased to live.

The bite in the back of the neck it was that killed the buffalo; the tiger had not had time to break its neck. His jaws had opened and released the neck—I watched them gasping—but the claws of his left paw had scarcely released the left side of the buffalo's cheek, so instantaneous had been his death.

All four feet of the tiger are beneath the body of the buffalo. They fell together.

I was well content to have successfully concluded my eighth night's vigil for this beast. His length was nine feet between pegs and his weight four hundred pounds, forearm 19 inches. Not a very big tiger, but of the ordinary size of those of these jungles. There was no sign of any former injury by bullet. The villagers were well pleased to be rid of this beast which had taken toll of their cattle for years and would still be doing so but for the pertinacious 'Nimrod'.

Now, the tiger is skinned and pegged out and I have told you all about him, I can hark back to tell you of other jungle affairs.

I often get up in the dark and hie off to the forests to see animals. I frequently saw sambur and four-horned antelope. Although the leaves are very dry, one can, by moving slowly and carefully, at the same time keeping the wind in the right direction, get quite close enough to see very well with the aid of field glasses. Where animals are seldom hunted, as is the case here, they are not so quick at detecting one as when they have been stalked and fired at.

Often, the sambur feed along quite unware that anyone is near them. The hinds with fawns keep separate from the stage. One stag I saw had fair horns—perhaps, 36 inches—and was exceptionally dark in colour. I have seen no stags anything approaching 40 inches and there is no doubt that to obtain a sambur head of such a size as to be of any value to a sportsman as a trophy, is a far more difficult undertaking than the killing of a tiger, unless of course, one happens to chance upon the beast on a fortunate occasion.

These forests seem to be overstocked with small stags; I see a great many. One day, several sambur came to within a few feet of me as I sat at the foot of a tree. Alas! My camera had been forgotten. When one gets on in years there is more desire to see than to destroy, and during the lives of the coming generation public opinion will more and more condemn the killing of wild animals. It is better to let live than to destroy, and the time is approaching when, if the hand of man is not stayed, there will be but few animals left to hunt! 'What about your own slayings?' you say. My answer is that my senile softness of heart does not extend to the greater carnivora; not yet at any rate!

Many people do not sit up at night, but to me there is a great charm about it. One learns to recognise the alarm calls of all the animals of the jungle; and the cries of the night birds, too. It was on one of those eight nights that I learnt to know the sound made by a porcupine; but whether he always makes the noise on his nightly wanderings, or whether this was a special occasion, I do not know. There was a loud expulsion and taking in of breath—such a noise as you can make for yourself by blowing out and inhaling quickly through your nose, doing it quickly—and I could not imagine what it could be. The tracks in the morning showed beyond any doubt what animal it was which had been puffing and blowing all around my tree.

I have wandered on and forgotten all about that panther story which I mentioned in the early part of this letter. It is in illustration of the want of fear evidenced by animals tethered in the forest as bait for the carnivora.

Sometimes, when one is dull in camp during the day, it is pleasant to take a book and ensconce oneself in a tree by a jungle pool, with a picketted goat to call up any panther which may be within hail. On one occasion—it was midday and the attendants had not gone a hundred yards—the bleating of the goat called up a panther from his siesta in a neighbouring ravine. He came trotting through the trees after the manner of an eager dog, halting for a second or so now and again as if he could hardly realise his good fortune at obtaining such an easy meal. Up to the goat he trotted, to be met by a lowered head. A feint of a lifted paw by the panther was countered by a butt from the fearless goat—the fearlessness of ignorance. Another feint by the panther, and in an instant he would have made the fatal attack: but his intention and his life were ended by a bullet in the chest. Down he sat exactly in his tracks, and as life-like as possible to the astonished goat which just sniffed at him and went on unconcernedly with his meal of thorn leaves. A panther without experience this and, though full grown, his weight of 100 lbs. for his length of 5 ft. 11 inches showed that he had not yet attained his full proportions; a young man just leaving college, in fact.

Now, we are packing up, our shikar in these parts at an end for the present, and in a couple of days will be a couple of hundred miles away, selves bound for a Hill Station and camp kit to be stored until again required. Such is the facility with which one can move about in these days of motor transport. Our one ton lorry is brought to our forest camp and takes all our belongings to destination for the very reasonable hire of eight annas a mile.

So, I end this long letter which takes to you a breath of the jungle—a pretty hot one just now!—and shall hope to give further history of our doings at some future time.

(1929)

The Panther and The Shepherd

By C.H. Donald

There are few places in India, where conditions permit, where the shepherds and panthers have not a bowing acquaintance with each other, but the Kangra Valley, with its huge range of mountains and valleys clothed in dense scrub and oak jungles, rather lends itself to this state of affairs.

During the bi-annual migration of sheep to and from their summer grazing grounds, panthers have a high old time and get fat, and the Guddis, on the other hand, tend to become lean from their nightly vigils and continual guard over their flocks.

You have only to ask a Guddi whether there are any panthers about and, if you are unacquainted with his ways, you will go away with the impression that life is not worth living and there are more panthers in the valley than there are goats and sheep, but that is only his little way of telling you that some damage has been done among his flocks. If you are a novice, and decide to take him at his word, and accept his invitation to visit his flock and sit up over a goat for the marauder who is doing untold damage, you will come away a sadder and wiser man without having seen so much as one spot of his glossy sleek coat.

Not that panthers are not there, but shepherds are everywhere when this migration begins and a panther can take his choice from among twenty or thirty flocks each night, and unless he is a fool, or extraordinarily attached to one flock, he makes a wide selection and range, and you might continue to sit over your goat for a week, while he kills everywhere except where you want him to. The shepherds, instead of helping you, do their best to hinder. They'll gladly give you a live goat to sit up over, knowing quite well that you'll pay for the goat if killed, and also *backshish* will be forthcoming if the panther is shot, but to give you *kubbar* of a freshly killed goat and to lead you thither is quite another matter. Often the goat, or sheep, is never found, but when it is, the Guddi thinks first of Number One, and that is himself. "That goat will be perfectly good to eat, but if the Sahib insists on sitting over it for a couple of nights, it certainly will not be, and who knows whether the panther will come and be shot or not, so let us take what the gods provide and eat the goat, and let the Sahib and the panther take their chance somewhere else." So says, and thinks the old Guddi, with the result that he will give you *kubbar* of a cow (which he does not eat), but never of a sheep or goat.

Should he, however, bring you notice of a goat that has been killed, you may be sure that what remains is neither fit for his consumption nor that of the felines and you can save yourself the trouble of going.

In spite of his knowledge of panthers and their ways, the Guddi is about the worst shikari you can find. Before I had had much experience of them, I gave them instructions to build a machan for me over a very freshly killed bullock, while I returned to have some lunch. They knew all about machans and had built hundreds, so they said, and I came away confident that I should get the panther that night. On my return, however, one glance at the tree and the machan, precluded the very smallest hope of anything but a blind panther coming near *that* kill. They had carefully cut down every branch and exposed the machan from every side, as they said, to enable me to get a good view all round. That the panther would also be able to get a good view of me from every side had never crossed their minds! Very occasionally a gun-possessed Guddi decides to sit up himself, and then he invites two or three pals to share his machan and his vigil with him, and they construct a platform on a tree which can be seen from half a mile, and come away next morning like martyrs in a good cause, because they have seen nothing. But, of course, there are Guddis and Guddis and there are a few exceptions to prove the rule, and some of them do occasionally shoot panthers. An amusing case came to my notice recently. A panther had done a good deal of damage in a village, so some half a dozen shepherds decided to take a share in building a trap for him. It took them several days' hard work collecting stones and it was really a fine structure they erected, and having wasted many days of their hard labour, the trap was never set, as they could not agree between them who should supply the kid to put into the trap as a bait!

A panther is an enigma. There are occasions when he proves himself to be the most cunning animal under the sun, and yet the very next day he will walk into an obvious trap that no self-respecting jackal would ever go near. One day a panther will prove himself to be an arrant coward and run like a hare from a couple of dogs, and the very next he will dash in among half a dozen men sitting round a camp fire, and remove a dog from their midst.

The "sawing" roar of the panther is frequently heard where these animals are to be found and one of the reasons given for this call is that the animal gives himself courage to approach a camp, by roaring lustily when he is still a little distance from it. Be this as it may, it (the call) is probably also a sexual one to give notice to its mate as to the animal's whereabouts, as it is sometimes heard miles away from any camp or village.

It is not often that one of these animals is taken by surprise, as both their marvellous powers of sight and hearing keep them amply warned, but very occasionally one might be seen sitting on a hill-top whence he can watch the surrounding country, or keep an eye on a flock of goats grazing near his domain, or some luckless village dog. Of course, he is a past master in the art of camouflage, and his spotted coat is admirably adapted for the purpose.

He does not need heavy jungle to hide him. A couple of bushes, and the light and shade from surrounding trees is quite enough to make him practically invisible and woe betide the individual who thinks he can follow up a wounded beast without taking every precaution.

The methods employed of shooting them is legion, but the most common is to sit up either over a kill or a live bait. Beating for him in the Punjab is usually most unsatisfactory, as one wants really experienced beaters to drive old "spots" out of his lair and thereafter conduct him to where the gun is waiting. The number of times he breaks back or slinks past some of the "stops" is incredible.

Leopards in love go out of their way to attract attention to themselves and seem to lose all sense of self-preservation, as the following little episode will show.

A man arrived one afternoon with the information that two panthers were fighting quite close to my house. Armed with a rifle I went off with him, and not a quarter of a mile away met a number of people standing on the road, a fairly well frequented road at that, looking at something up the hill. On one side there were 30 to 40 cattle grazing and just beyond a flock of sheep. "Here is the place" announced the Guddi who came with the information, and hardly had he spoken when somebody said "look, Sahib, look!" I looked and at that moment a panther sprang from a rock and disappeared into a cave, and was followed by a frightful hullabaloo inside. "They have been going on like this all day" remarked one of the onlookers.

They were not fifty yards above the road where the crowd (some 15 or 20 men and women) was standing. I climbed up the spur and took up a position some 20 yards from the cave and straight opposite it, among some boulders, and had not to wait five minutes before one animal appeared a few yards below the cave and jumped on to a bolder in plain view. I fired and it toppled over into the rocks below without a sound. I waited for half an hour or so for the other but he did not put in an appearance, so leaving a couple of men to watch I went home to have some tea, and thereafter returned to see if I could make better acquaintance with the gentleman in the cave, and waited for an hour or so after sending away the men. He showed up but not till the light had almost gone and I could not make him out over the sights of my rifle as he blended so beautifully with the fallen oak leaves. After two or three vain efforts to pick out his head and neck from the leaves and rocks, he saw me and sprang clear into some brushwood and was gone.

The advent of the Kangra Valley Railway and the influx of sportsmen into this peaceful vale will, in time, bring peace to the Guddi and his flocks, but it will be a long time ere panthers are reduced to any appreciable extent in this land of forests and rocks which supply such excellent cover for the wily pard.

(1928)

Indian Lions

By C.A. Kincaid

The Indian lion should be one of the unhappiest beasts alive! It is the firm belief of every Englishman, impressed on him in the nurseries of England, that the Indian lion is a mangy, maneless brute; and as he rarely sees one he dies with this belief firmly implanted in his breast. This belief is the grossest of libels upon the animal in question. It in no way differs from its cousin of North Africa. It is, it is true, smaller than the lion of South Africa, an immense beast, but it is every bit as big as the Somali lion and has a splendid mane. This hirsute decoration is often combed off if its owner lives in the forest; but the same fate happens to the African lion. Put both in captivity and the Indian will grow as big a mane as any lion of East or West Africa. Fortunately gross although the libel be, the Indian lion knows nothing of it and is thus saved from much mental pain and misery.

The Indian lion once roamed over the whole of India. In the early Sanskrit fables we hear a great deal about lions but nothing about tigers. The reason is that the tiger is a new-comer. Its home was in Manchuria and there it grew and still grows a fine thick fur. Like the Mongols, its neighbours, the tiger cast an envious look on the rich plains of India and descended on them. It drove the lion completely out of Bengal and then out of northern and southern India. When the English came, the lion was still holding out against the invader in central India, Guzarat and Kathiawar; but the English completed the lion's defeat. It was exterminated in the two former provinces and its only refuge left is in Junagadh, a State in Kathiawar, where there are no tigers and where H.H. the Nawab preserves the lion against English sportsmen.

I have not visited the Gir forest for more than twenty years, so I do not know what its present boundaries are. I believe a good deal of it has since then been cut down but twenty-five years ago it was a very extensive reserve. It began less than twelve miles from the seaport of Verawal and stretched northward to within a few miles of Junagadh. It was full of sambhur, chital and panther and it sheltered about a hundred and fifty lions. As there was not enough game to keep these lions fed, they preyed on the cultivator's cattle and goats and not infrequently on the cultivators themselves. They had no fear of man; for they saw the foresters move through the forest every day and they were never hunted save when His Highness wished to entertain a Viceroy or a Governor of Bombay or when they had developed too violent a passion for human flesh. They were extraordinarily long lived. They lived usually forty years and some were even believed to live to the age of seventy; as they were prolific, they would rapidly have spread over the countryside but for certain causes. If any lion strayed outside Junagadh limits, it was at the mercy of any chief or sahib who came to hear of it. The foresters, whenever they came across a brood of lion cubs unattended by their parents, invariably attacked them with axes. Lastly, the Junagadh State needed a constant supply of young lion cubs for its fine zoological gardens. My first experience of the Indian lion was in those gardens. I went with other English visitors into a square, around which were small cages such as are still seen in travelling circuses. These were filled with lions and as it was just before their dinner hour, they were making the most awful noise. I was feeling rather frightened when an Indian gentleman said to me that the cages had been recently reported to be unsafe. I was seized with a wild panic and would gladly have run out of the grounds; fortunately the presence of other visitors restrained me and in time I got quite accustomed to the noise. The lions in the 'zoo' were mostly friendly; their keeper had taught them various tricks which they like to practise. But there were two male lions that were divided by an inextinguishable hatred. They had been friends and had been brought up in the same cage. A certain day—it was probably a hot and liverish day—one of the lions could no longer stand the angle at which the other carried its tail. It went up to its companion and without warning bit its tail off. The tail—I saw part of the incident myself—lay long and stiff on the floor of the cage, while all round it the tailless one and the wicked one fought a fearful battle. They were separated with the greatest difficulty and forced into separate cages; but they never forgot their hatred and whenever one caught the other's eye it would roar volley after volley of leonine abuse at it.

Another lion had had an interesting experience; it had escaped from its cage a year or two before I saw it. Now, the young lion has to learn its lesson just like young Englishmen or young Indians. Unless it is taught by its mother to stalk and kill game it never knows how to do so. The lion of which I am writing had been caught when quite tiny and had never learnt how to procure its food. When it escaped from the Junagadh gardens it took by instinct the road to the Gir forest, but once in the shelter of the woods it had no idea what to do. Dinner hour passed but no kindly keeper brought dinner. It tried to stalk a sambhur but its clumsy efforts only excited the stag's contempt. It tried to seize a goat but the herdsmen drove it off with stones. At the same time its feet were getting dreadfully sore. Its pads had only been used to the smooth bottom of its cage; they were cut to pieces by the stones of the road and the thorns of the forest. It would have very soon died of starvation. Fortunately the keeper of the zoological gardens was experienced in recovering runaways. He put a portable cage on a bullock cart and with it and two bullocks he set out into the jungle. When he entered it, he began calling to the lion in a way that he had previously done when bringing its dinner. The joyful sound came to the fugitive's ears, just as it was about to give up hope, and gave it new strength. Pulling itself together, it ran towards the keeper. Seeing the cage that reminded it of the flesh pots of Egypt, it had no thought of attacking the bullocks. With a roar of thanksgiving it leapt through the open door of the cage and threw itself on the meat that lay inside all ready for it. While it was so engaged the keeper shut the door and turning the bullock cart brought back the runaway in triumph to Junagadh. The lion when I saw it seemed greatly attached to the keeper and probably never again longed for freedom.

My first meeting with a wild lion was in 1902 when I was spending the hot weather at Verawal; I had got leave to shoot panther in the Gir from His Highness the then Nawab and *khabar* of panther at Tellala was brought to me when I was in tents on the seashore of that charming little Junagadh port. I sent my tents to Tellala, a little village on the banks of the Hiran river and one of the most beautiful spots I have seen. The Hiran river was, during the hot weather, full of water partly because of the low dam at Verawal and partly because of a strange natural phenomenon, which so far as I know was unique. At the end of every monsoon the sea threw up a barrier of sand that blocked the mouth of the Hiran river three miles from Verawal. The result was that during eight months of the year a fresh water lake was formed on the very edge of the sea and the Hiran river bed all through the hot weather was full of water. The first day that I arrived at Tellala I went out with a shikari and sat until dark on a tree waiting in vain for the panther to be tempted by my bait. When I could no longer see my foresight I told the shikari that it was useless to wait any more; we climbed down and started for Tellala. About a mile from the camp, we were suddenly aware that a band of lions (I counted four, my shikari counted six) was walking towards us up the high road. We stopped at a loss what to do. The lions came towards us, apparently for some time unaware of us. When they saw us they stopped also; and then we stood looking at each other, both sides evidently disconcerted. I could not shoot, as I had promised not to kill a lion unless absolutely forced to in self-defence. The lions evidently thought that I and the shikari and our two or three beaters were too big a party to attack. I do not know how long we stood face to face. It seemed a very long time to me, but was probably not more than ten minutes. Then we heard shouts and saw torches, moving towards us. The lions did not like the situation. They got restive and I thought that they were going to charge us and I got ready to shoot. But they slowly moved off the road into the jungle. As they did so my servants and several villagers came up shouting and carrying torches and joined us. We could see the lions a few yards off the road and we walked past them, glad at having out-manoeuvred them. Had not my servants and the villagers very pluckily taken the lions in the rear, we probably should have had to fight and the fight might well have gone against us. The lions were not satisfied with the result. Two nights later the same band came close to my tent and started roaring furiously. I had a pony with me and they hoped by roaring to frighten it and make it bolt into the jungle. Had it done so, they would soon have caught it up and eaten it; but it was an affectionate little Arab and so long as I sat by it and petted and stroked it, it felt sure that I would keep it safe against all the world. I stayed by it until three in the morning. By that time the lions had moved off and I was able to get a few hours' sleep.

The Agent to the Governor, my old and valued friend Colonel Kennedy, C.S.I., had about the same time a curious experience. Going into the Gir not long after me, he was sitting over a goat in the hope of getting a panther, when a large maned lion came up to the "bait" and taking it in its mighty jaws walked off with it, much as a retriever does with a running pheasant. Colonel Kennedy shouted at the lion and threw branches at it, but it only snarled at him contemptuously and went its way, taking the Colonel's goat with it.

I got my first chance at a lion three years later. In 1905, Lord Lamington, then Governor of Bombay, came to Rajkot on an official visit and afterwards went on the invitation of the Nawab of Junagadh to shoot in the Gir. His camp was at Shashan in the very heart of the Gir. The Governor and some of his staff went in one direction and his Private Secretary, Mr D—, a young soldier and Major Carnegy, the political officer, went in another. I saw poor Carnegy off at the station and was much concerned to hear him say that he had only a light sporting rifle. He, however, assured me that he did not mean to shoot. What led him to shoot in the end I do not know. An extra gun was probably needed; anyway he went out with the Private Secretary's party.

Beats were organised and Mr D—wounded a lion as it passed him. Now, the rule of the jungle for all sportsmen is that wounded big game must be followed up and killed; otherwise they prey on the villagers. The three Englishmen followed the lion and came up with it. It charged and knocking down Carnegy bit his head and broke his skull. Mr D—killed the lion as it stood over its victim; but it was too late. Carnegy was already dead.

It was a dreadful tragedy but it did me a good turn. Realising that after this accident the Gir lions would be rather unpopular, I ventured a month later to ask His Highness if I might shoot a lion before saying good-bye to Kathiawar, which I was likely to leave shortly. To my delight the reply was in the affirmative. My wife and I went to Verawal to spend the hot weather. At Easter we took our tents to Tellala. As it happened, one of the lions there had become a bad man-eater and I was especially asked to kill it, if I could. The Gir foresters' method of marking down a lion is worthy of record. They know as a rule all the lions in their part of the forest and their habits. When they are required to produce one, they follow it about all night preventing it from either eating or killing. In the morning it is exhausted and crawls into a thicket to sleep through the day. The foresters then hoist a cot to the top of a tree and a quarter a mile away surround the thicket on all sides except one, send for the favoured hunter, and when he is seated in his cot, drive the lion past him. The object of the cot is not to conceal the hunter, but to give him a good view of the jungle near him and keep him out of the way of the lion. A lion like other beasts of prey is not an "anthropos" and therefore does not look upwards unless it is wounded. Were the hunter on foot and blocking the lion's exit he would certainly be charged. In a tree the lion takes no notice of him.

On arrival at Tellala I showed my "parwana" or permit to the head forester, who at once made his dispositions to get me a lion. He did not know where the man-eater was for the moment but he knew of two full-grown lions close to our camp. He followed them all that night. We got no news next morning and we were beginning to fear we should get no shooting that day. At midday, to our delight, a man came with news that the lions had been marked down about two miles from Tellala. We were to set out a little before two o'clock.

About 1-45, my wife, who refused to be left behind, and I mounted our horses and followed our guide through the most lovely forest scenery that I have ever seen. A quarter of a mile from our station, the head forester met us and bade us dismount and follow him. We did so and walked through glades and rides until we came to the tree where the cot had been hoisted. My wife, the head forester and I got into it, and a man was sent to start the beat. About half an hour, we knew by the sound of distant shouting that the beat had begun. It came nearer and nearer in an infernal crescendo. Just when it seemed as if Hell itself had been let loose, I saw what seemed a shadow flit through some bushes thirty yards off. My wife saw it too and touched my arm. A second later a splendid lioness walked out of the cover, as angry as any beast that I have ever seen. Her tail stood out behind as stiff as a ramrod and her eyes had a most unpleasant expression. I did not fire as she came towards the tree for if I had only wounded her, she would have seen us on the cot and she could easily have leapt up and swept us off with a blow of her paw. When she had passed, I fired behind her shoulder. The high velocity bullet hit her a little low. She fell down twisted round and struggled to her feet. I fired again into her back and hit her spine. She rolled into a bush and just then the beaters came up.

The male lion had broken back and they thought that I had fired at it. They began saying what a pity it was. I reassured them, however, as to my skill as a marksman and told them in Guzarati that a wounded lioness was lying close to their feet. On hearing this, they stood not upon the order of their going, they went at once. And, in a moment every tree in the neighbourhood bore its load of agonised beaters, who were striving to reach the summit.

On returning to camp I sent a letter to His Highness the Nawab informing him that I had shot a lioness and that my wife had gone with me to the shoot and thanking him for the very great pleasure that we owed to his kindness. Early next morning I got the most delightful telegram that I have ever received "Take lioness for Madam Sahib, get lion for yourself." I showed it to the head forester who at once set about getting me a male lion. By a stroke of fortune, he was able to locate the bad man-eater, who was said to have accounted for no less than twenty-eight herdsmen and cultivators. The forester followed him up all that night and next day about noon we received word that the man-eating lion had been marked down about six miles away. A good road ran most of the distance, so my wife and I drove very comfortably through beautiful woods until we were met by the head forester. He made us, as before, walk for about a quarter of a mile until we came to where our cot awaited us. We climbed into it and the beat began as before. When the beaters had come near us, there suddenly rushed out of cover three quarter grown lion cubs. They were the most ridiculous objects imaginable; they rolled over each other playing like bull-terrier puppies. I got so excited that I would have shot one, only the head forester restrained me. After staying under my tree for a minute or so they scampered off; then at the last moment the man-eater sprang out of cover and dashed across in open space. It was a wily old campaigner and had evidently sent out its four young ones to draw the fire of any lurking enemies. I took rather rashly a snapshot at it, as it galloped past. A lucky shot broke its spine and it collapsed. It was a noble beast but its canine teeth had been broken and it was that misfortune probably that had led it to take exclusively to human diet.

So ended my connexion with the Gir lion but my good fortune continued all those holidays. A day or two later I got a panther and the same evening I received a letter from the Private Secretary to Lord Lamington informing me that I had been promoted to be judge of Poona. I was extremely pleased and wrote in great joy to my people at home. My proud parents told a somewhat serious friend; to their surprise he did not rejoice with them. He murmured in shocked tones "Good Heavens! Did your son shoot the judge of Poona, too?"

(1928)

Some Panthers

By C.A. Kincaid

I cannot pretend to be in any sense of the word a big game shot; but I have been out a good many times after panthers. Since some of my experiences with them were rather exciting, I think that they might interest the readers of the *Indian State Railways Magazine*.

Kathiawar when I first knew it thirty years ago simply swarmed with panthers. There was a panther to be found on every hill and in almost every thicket. It was no uncommon occurrence to go out after black buck and to come back with a couple of buck and a panther lying dead in the same bullock cart. Colonel Fenton, while in Kathiawar, killed over eighty of them and several men whom I knew had speared them as if they had been pigs. The cause of the multitude of these *dipras* was no doubt the disordered state of the country. Only a few years before I was posted to Kathiawar, the province was overrun with bands of dacoits. They were generally led by some unfortunate landowner, who had been dispossessed of his estate by a none too scrupulous overlord. If he could escape capture long enough, he generally got his claims settled. If he was captured, he was shot out of hand. But as every small landowner in Kathiawar was in danger immediate or remote of dispossession, his sympathy and his secret help were always given to the man who had "left the path" as the Gujarati phrase went and had become a *bahirwatia* or outlaw. The bands of dacoits levied blackmail everywhere and robbed unfortunate shopkeepers or merchants or even rich cultivators whom they caught, mercilessly. The result was that village after village was deserted and left untilled; and panthers made their homes in what had once been cultivated areas.

To return, however, to the subject of my article, my first panther is the one that I shall always remember most vividly. No doubt because it was my first, but also because it gave me more trouble than any other. I had obtained permission to shoot a panther in the Gir forest from the Junagadh authorities and armed with a new .400 Jeffery high velocity rifle that I just had built for me, I went off gaily to the Gir. I first tried Tellala, a favourite spot for panthers, but my chief, Colonel Kennedy, had just bagged a brace there and there were no others for the moment. The Junagadh authorities, who were always kindness itself to British officers, arranged that I should go to another part of the Gir, a village known, so far as I remember, as Gurmukhwadi.

When I arrived at my camp at my destination, I found tents in great numbers and furnished with every regard to my comfort. My servants were highly excited, because they had passed lions on the way from Tellala. However, no damage had been done and after listening to their highly varnished tale, I asked whether there had been a kill. A tall shikari, who had been listening to the servants' tale with some contempt, stepped forward and said that a panther had killed a peasant's goat early that morning and would probably return that afternoon to feed on it. Would the

Sahib sit up for it? The Sahib said with much eagerness that he would sit up for it. Then the shikari said with perfect frankness: "Shooting panthers, Sahib, is different from shooting hares. Will the Sahib kindly shoot at a mark and shew me whether he can hit anything?" It was impossible to take offence at the man's words. He spoke with such dignity. I accordingly fired at a mark and apparently satisfied him; for he went away saying he would return at four and take me to the kill.

The hours passed very slowly, but at last four struck and the shikari appeared. We rode about two miles, dismounted near a small woodland village and walked a few hundred yards to where a machan or stand had been built over the remains of the unfortunate goat. It was not long before the shikari gave me a nudge to let me know that the panther was somewhere about. I do not know what he had seen, nor did I dare ask him, for I was too excited. He must have caught a glimpse of the panther, for a few minutes later a female panther stepped out of some undergrowth and sitting down like a dog began to call. My shikari wanted me to wait; but it was my first panther and I could not wait. What if the brute should bolt while I waited for it to come nearer. Regardless of the shikari, I put up my rifle and although I was very awkwardly placed for my aim, I fired. The high velocity bullet missed the panther's chest and struck it in the hindleg. It swung round twice in a circle and vanished in the undergrowth instantly.

The next question was what was to be done. Before I had left India, several persons, who had shot in other parts of India, had warned me against the danger of following a wounded tiger or panther on foot. "Always wait for your elephant", they said. But in the Bombay Presidency there are no elephants. For that contingency my Mentors had not provided; and as it is impossible to leave a wounded panther at large to kill the villagers, I had to descend sadly from my tree and start following the wounded beast on foot. I must confess that as I walked, I wondered why I had ever been so foolish as to go out panther shooting. I was not only concerned about myself, but about the villagers. They had come out in great numbers and armed, as all villagers in native states are with swords, they threw caution to the winds. One man got on to the panther's trail and shouting out "Am avyo" (He has come this way), he ran off at full speed on the panther's tracks.

Unhappily the villager was on the right trail and, while I ran after him as quickly as I could, he came to where the wounded panther lay. It charged straight at him and knocking him over, tried to get at his throat. He held it off long enough for a young Rajput to draw his sword and give it a tremendous cut across the head. It left its intended victim and ran into a little bush close by. I had by this time come up and was shewn the wounded panther. It was lying down, but was wagging its tail like an angry cat. Again wondering why I had ever had the foolish wish to go out panther shooting, I drew a bead on the back of the wounded beast's neck. It was the most visible part of its body. The high velocity bullet this time hit its mark fair and square. The tail wagging ceased and the panther was dead. Much of my pleasure at my first panther was spoilt by the injury to the rash villager. Fortunately it was not serious. I had the man sent to the nearest hospital. In a few days he was perfectly well again; but I fancy that he treated panthers in future with more respect.

The most daring panther that I remember was one I shot some years later in the same Gir forest. My wife and I were camped by the sea side at Verawal, when a forester came and complained that there was a very bold panther near where he lived, would the Sahib come and shoot it. We were going into the Gir just then after lions, so I could do nothing at the time; but while camped in the Gir, I found a day to attend to the bold panther. One afternoon my wife and I started out on horse back followed by a shikari leading a wretched she-goat. Near the machan, we had to dismount and cross some very wild country. Once arrived at the machan, events moved very quickly. We climbed into our tree, the beaters tied up the goat, and as they left called to it. As the form of the last man moved round a rock the head of a panther came round a rock, on the other side. The brute was not in the least afraid of men and, so we heard afterwards, had several times carried off goats on a lead.

The panther was a little far off for a perfectly safe shot, so I waited. The goat had been calling cheerfully to its human friends when it suddenly saw the panther a few yards away. It became petrified with terror and made no further sound. It walked to the end of its cord and gazed as if hypnotised at the monster, whose dinner it was to provide. The panther did not seem hungry. It slowly sat down like a huge tomcat and watched with quiet enjoyment the emotions it was rousing in the goat's breast. I on the other hand was growing more and more excited. I felt that if I waited much longer, my hand would tremble, so that I should not be able to aim straight. I drew a bead on the brute's chest, as it faced me. I pulled the trigger and the panther rolled over growling helplessly. My second barrel hit it in the body and all motion stopped. I had hardly fired my second barrel, when my men came running back very much surprised to hear the shots so soon. We descended and we found that my first bullet had hit the panther higher than I had intended. The bullet had struck it straight between the eyes. To use the expression of my shikari, I had given it a *chanllo* or sect mark. No other incident followed save the almost unendurable swagger of the unharmed goat on the return journey. It was clear to its mind at any rate that it alone "had won the War".

Another very bold panther came into my tents when I was in Mahableshwar. Our bull-terrier bitch had presented us with a litter of puppies, which would have served admirably for a healthy panther's supper. The mother had the courage of her race and although chained to one of the tentpoles, kept up so fierce a growling that the servants heard her and drove away the panther in time. The same day I learnt that the panther had been seen in the Blue Valley Road, which was quite close. At the suggestion of a local shikari, I went the same evening with a goat in the hope of getting a shot. On the way we met the panther. It was in no way disconcerted, but just stepped aside to let us pass. I could see it faintly in the undergrowth, but not clearly enough to fire. We decided to go on and sit up just off the Blue Valley Road. We tied up our goat and waited for an hour or so. It was now so dark that it was useless to wait any longer, so we decided to go back, leaving the goat there. Next morning the shikari reported that the goat had been killed and advised my sitting up for the panther the same afternoon. My wife insisted on coming too; and at five o'clock we were in the machan. We had a longish wait, for carriages were passing along the road; and last of all an idiotic Member of Council who had never done any shooting himself, passed by with his wife. Seeing the goat, he went up to it and not seeing us began to tell his wife all about the shoot that would shortly take place. We condemned him to all sorts of hot places while he talked and we sighed with relief when he passed on. The panther, who had probably been as bored by the Member's talk as we had been, waited only a few minutes longer. Suddenly it galloped across an open space almost noiselessly, looked up and down the road to see if any more carriages were coming and then walked with leisurely step to the kill. I fired between its shoulders and it sank without a struggle.

On another occasion at Mahableshwar, I had an experience that I had some difficulty in getting my friends to believe. A panther kill was reported about three miles beyond the Robbers' Cave. I rode out there, reaching the spot about half past four, as the panther was expected to return early. When I reached the spot I found the men, who were watching the kill in some excitement. The panther had already returned, and they had had some difficulty in chasing it back into the woods. After this tale, I hardly expected to see the animal again. But the country was very wild. The lords of the jungle had no fear of man; and I had hardly seated myself comfortably in the machan, when the shikari nudged me. Looking in the direction where he pointed, I could just make out through the undergrowth a panther lying like a cat and switching away flies with its tail. There was no chance of a safe shot for the moment, so with a heart hammering with excitement, I waited on events. Suddenly the brute vanished and I wondered where it had gone. I looked towards the kill, but it had not gone there. I turned to the shikari and saw him shaking with terror. "He is coming to attack us" he whispered. I could see nothing whatever of the animal and wondered whence the attack would be launched. For some time I could get no sense out of the man. At last he pointed to a branch of the next tree and above our heads. There, like a cat on the back of an armchair, was the panther. It had apparently climbed up the tree and in doing so had scared the shikari. Quite ignorant of our presence it was looking at the kill, waiting for its appetite to improve. I at first hesitated to shoot, for I feared that I might knock the panther on the top of us. Then I calculated that it would miss us and aiming carefully, fired.

Instantaneously the animal slid down its own tree and missed us with a good deal to spare. It was only about ten feet off when I fired and it was dead before it reached the ground.

Sometimes one had to go very far afield at Mahableshwar for one's panther. One day in the second week in June when the rains begin to fall, I got *khabar* of a panther in the valley beyond the Krishna. There was a drop of two thousand feet into the Krishna valley, a climb of two thousand feet the other side and then a drop of two thousand feet into the valley next to it. I started at two in the afternoon from my bungalow. As we reached the brow of the plateau and began to descend, we passed a little image of Ganpati and the hillmen all *salaamed* to it, because Ganpati is the god who blesses all beginnings. The author who begins to write a new book, the banker who opens a new ledger, the traveller who starts on a voyage all invoke the kindly help of Ganpati. Then we dropped down the steep path amid pouring rain, then up the other side and then down the hill again. Fortunately the rain stopped and I climbed into my machan. I was wet to the skin, but my clothes dried rapidly in the sun and I was cheered by the sound of a panther calling a few hundred yards away. I wanted a drink badly, but the shikari had no pity and made me settle in my machan. "There will be lots of time to drink, Sahib" he said, "when you have killed the panther". To this austere view I had to agree, as there was always the danger, that the panther, near as it was, might see us.

It was a long wait. The panther kept calling for an hour, but came no nearer. Then a long silence followed. I grew impatient. I said to the shikari, "It's no use waiting any longer, is it?" He put his finger to his lips and said one word *Yell* (it will come). I grumbled no more. The kill was the body of a young heifer. The panther had dragged its victim's corpse under a high rock, that stood up about twenty yards from where I was hidden. I looked so long and earnestly at the kill and the rock, that I must have hypnotised myself into a doze. I woke up with a start, as the shikari touched my shoulder and whispered *"Ala"* (it has come). I gripped my rifle, looked all round but could see nothing. It was dusk and it was getting difficult to notice objects. Then I noticed what seemed to be a round stone on the top of the rock opposite me. I had not observed it before and I wondered whether it could be a portion of a panther. It seemed, however, to be motionless. Just as I was about to look elsewhere, the round rock began to grow and then alter its shape, and I at last made out clearly the head and forequarters of a panther. It looked enormous in the fading light and I confess that I thought it was a tiger.

Slowly the wary beast pulled itself to its feet and began to walk round the side of the great rock. For a second it disappeared, and I was in an agony of apprehension that it had gone for ever. I wondered how on earth I should climb back all those thousands of feet after a blank day. Then it reappeared and I was all excitement again. Very slowly and silently, it walked across the face of the rock until it was just over the dead heifer. "Maro Sahib" (Shoot), whispered my shikari and I aimed as best I could; for it had got so dark that I could barely make out the foresight. I f ired and was very pleased to see my enemy crumple up and fall over. I still hoped that it might be a tiger and I joyously descended from my tree after giving the prone object a second barrel. The beaters would have rushed up to the dead animal, but I was able to keep them by me. We walked up to it, I covering it with my rifle. At last one of the beaters bent forward and pulled the animal's tail. It made no response. "It is dead, Sahib," said the shikari. "No *wagh* would suffer such an insult were it alive". The shikari was right. It was dead, but it was only a panther.

I had my drink, while the beaters tied the panther's feet to a bamboo. Then with our enemy ignominiously hanging upside down from the bamboo, we started homewards. At the frontier of every village, the beaters shouted to the village god that they had killed a panther and that the god should rejoice. We climbed up two thousand feet, then walked down two thousand feet into the Krishna valley. The stream was lit up in the weirdest way. The whole population of the valley were engaged in catching the crabs that infest the river bed and damage the crops. All of them had torches in their hands. These, I was told, dazzled the crabs. In any case they gave the hunters a chance of seeing their quarry. I watched them for some time and then started to climb the last two thousand feet to the brow of the Mahableshwar plateau. I shall never forget that climb. It was raining again. I had had no tea and no dinner. By the time I reached the top, I was "dead to the world". And when we passed the little image of Ganpati, I, this time, *salaamed* before any one else!

It was 2 a.m. by the time I found my tonga on the road. Into it we stuffed the panther; and as I drove off I heard the beaters singing and laughing as they raced down the steep hill paths. Fatigue and they had never met.

The next summer I got a second panther in very nearly the same place, only a hundred feet up the far side of the valley. It was a bold panther this time, so the shikari told me, and it would not keep me waiting long. It had, it seemed, early that morning rushed past a herdsman, pulled down one of his young cows in spite of his loudly vocal protests. The other herdsmen had come up and had driven the robber off his prey and word had been sent to Mahableshwar. I received the news from my shikari and again I went down two thousand feet and up two thousand feet and down two thousand feet and then up a hundred feet the other side. The kill lay out in the open and the trees round were villagers squatting like vultures. They had had a hard time keeping the panther off the kill.

I got into my machan, loaded my rifle and settled myself comfortably. Then I looked round. It was the wildest spot that I had ever been in. Rough, low scrub covered the hill side and hid the coarse grass beneath. There was not a sign of human dwelling visible, although there must have been huts somewhere in which the herdsmen lived. I felt thankful that good actions done in some former life had saved me from a life spent in such a valley. Then I looked at the kill and at the bushes round it. As I did so, a beautifully marked panther walked fearlessly into the open. It stood still and looked to see if the herdsmen, who had previously driven it off its prey were still there. Seeing and hearing nothing, it turned to take a step nearer the kill. I put up my rifle and aimed. As I did so, my sight protector came off the barrel and fell to the ground. I passed an agonising moment. If the sight protector had struck a rock, the noise would have startled the panther and I should never have been seen again. Happily the sight protector fell in the grass and made no sound. A second later I had fired and the panther was dead. It was a beautiful beast and I was delighted to get the skin. The tramp back was severe, but less so than on the previous occasion. It was much earlier in the day and I was back for dinner.

I went several times afterwards into the Krishna and adjoining valleys, but without any fortune. One day, however, I had an interesting experience. I had climbed down into the Krishna valley and up the other side and there I sat over the kill. It was a young bull that had been slain that morning by a panther, said by the villagers to have developed man-eating tendencies. I waited until it was dark and then got out of the machan. To light us homewards, one of the beaters carried a lantern. Just before we got to the edge of the plateau and were about to descend into the Krishna valley, the lantern bearer stopped and pointed to the ground. We came up and looked. Over the footprints that we had left as we walked towards the machan were the footprints of the panther. As we stalked it, it had stalked us, and had we not been such a large party, it might have tried to carry one of us off. It was very interesting and I was almost consoled for my blank day. I have always had a soft spot in my heart for that panther. We did each other no injury; we parted as friends. I did not get the panther and better still it did not get me.

(1928)

An Adventure with a Tigress

By N.B. Mehta

T·alking of lions reminds me of a remarkable experience I had with a tigress in the forests of the Central Provinces. "Remarkable", inasmuch as I am still a piece of humanity journeying on with the great caravan—obviously for some important mission—and not stray molecules floating in the flesh and blood of a Berar man-eater. Every man has a few notable reminiscences to narrate in company when the conversation lags or when some youthful spirit in the style of Falstaff—may his soul rest in peace—narrates how single-handed he withstood, nay frustrated, the onslaught of half a dozen warriors, or how he measured in dust a wily panther in a dark deep Indian forest. This is my modest tale of adventure.

It came about in this wise. I, in company of two other officers was deputed to survey the traffic prospects of a railway line in the Central Provinces and had meandered into Akot, a station on the proposed railway, and a considerable cotton centre, twenty-eight miles to the north of Akola. We had halted at the *dak* bungalow, that oasis in the Indian countryside, when we were informed that the great attraction thereabouts was a hill fortress, Narnala, fourteen miles northward to be reached by car. We were no tourists and yet, as the next official move-on was to take place the next afternoon, we decided—a companion and I—to visit the fort and appreciate the best mediæval Afghan architecture thereon. Strange is human wanderlust!

Half-past-five the next morning found us starting for Narnala. We disdained to wait for the guide kindly arranged for by the local *Vahivatdar*. We could see the hill and the faint outlines of the fortress from the *dak* bungalow. And what is visible dispels fear. Again had we not tramped twelve miles through a trackless forest in the Melaghat under a blazing sun, crossing the Tapti bare-footed and brought back in four hours information and statistics concerning the traffic potentialities of a jungle station? So we left with confidence. The car stopped at the foot of the hill and alighting we strode briskly towards our destination, which loomed high above. It was an April morning, cool and bracing, and we had no doubt but that in an hour's time we would scale the hill and reach the fortress, although we had no guide and we had but a hazy notion of the way up. Two miles we raced thus treading lightly on the crisp forest leaves. Once or twice we felt we were not going in the right direction, but we were undaunted and hoped to reach our goal somehow. Then the thing happened. We were approaching an open space with a miserable bush to the right and a few bare silver birch-like trees to the left when, with a repeating growl, a huge Bengal tigress leaped barely eight yards in front of us. It was a beautiful clean jump and we should have applauded it in a circus show. But what was still more surprising was the repeating snarling noise which she emitted. No, it was not a roar that reverberates in a forest and I don't know why she preferred this method of welcoming us except that we looked, armed as we were with a cane and a camera, meek and modest, and she thought it better to reserve her loud speaker for a more fitting occasion. Then instead of leaping on us and giving us the *coup de grace* she described a semi-circle with her snarling face towards us and disappeared in the same bush. We were non-plussed at this uncalled for visitation and acting on the instinct of self-preservation, we picked up a few stones and started to run in the opposite direction. This was just the thing not to do; for on her return visit she could have caught us in a couple of leaps. Luckily I remembered having read that tigers don't climb trees and acting upon this, I instructed my companion to climb one of the small slender trees that were about us. I also lost no time in swinging up on one.

Hardly had we done so before the tigress with the same old semi-humorous growl rushed at us through the thicket and stared at us with surprise. But she was now frustrated. Why she did not knock us down when we were on *terra firma* quietly walking towards her is to me an unsolved riddle. It may be that she was afraid of the safety of her two cubs, who, we subsequently learnt, were with her, and went back into the thicket to assure herself of their safety. Whatever the cause of her clumsy mistake at our first meeting, at the second we were safely perched on the branches of two trees beyond her reach and contemplating her exasperation with good humour.

Once temporarily safe, we began to consider the means we should take to escape the attention of the beast who was all the time hiding in the thicket and waiting for us to come down. One thing was certain: we must escape and reach the village where our car was awaiting us and that before darkness set in. And we realised that as we were surrounded by tall hills on all sides it would be dark by 4 p.m. It was not particularly cold but it was blowing frightfully. Starvation was not our dread as we had stuffed our pockets with biscuits.

The nearest village was two miles away and as we had strayed off the beaten track the chances of people coming in our direction were remote. I then resorted to shouting at intervals of ten minutes in the hope of drawing the attention of some passer-by. We were on the tree for quite an hour before my shout received a reply. Two shikaris with guns and our chauffeur then turned up and we knew we were saved. The shikaris heard our story and asked us the direction in which the beast had gone. We followed her footsteps but evidently she had taken a fortified position among the rocks and we thought it best to turn back to the village. We followed the footprints of the tigress towards the village where she had gone the previous evening and we came across stray limbs of a buffalo, a tell-tale evidence of the beast's previous meal. The shikaris also pointed out to us the smaller footprints of the two cubs. We certainly thanked our gods that the fate of the buffalo did not befall us. I suspect it was the sumptuous meal which the tigress and her cubs had had on the buffalo which made our visitor reluctant to draw the blood of such ignoble adversaries, as we were.

(1928)

The Midnight Visitor

By C.A. Renny

All day long the air had glowed with a shimmering, unbearable heat. Long since the Christmas rains had departed and none other had fallen, the grassy levels of the plain surrounding my temporary abode and coolie lines were scorched and yellow, while gaping cracks, cleft in the ground by days of pitiless heat, were a menace to cattle by day and roving animals at night. The mango, sal and simul stood covered with hot dust hurled up by an occasional whirlwind, their dry and tired leaves drooping and thirsty, waiting for the rain that would not come.

It was the end of June, yet there were no signs of the approach of the monsoon. Nightly to south-westward, the sky was lit up by occasional flashes of summer lightning. All day, the work of transplanting went on with no sign of pleasure, the usual songs of the coolies as they worked, a sure sign of contentment, were hushed; all were contriving to complete the task set them as soon as possible to get home under the shelter of their thatched roofs.

The thermometer for days now had registered a hundred degrees, and the humid atmosphere of the Darjeeling Tarai made life as unbearable and uncomfortable as it could possibly be.

Extra work in the evening was out of the question, to expect it was inhumane.

About four o'clock in the afternoon, the neighbouring garden assistant rode over for a chat and a cup of tea. "Gee whizz," he exclaimed as he slid out of his saddle. "Today beats all other days and if tomorrow beats today, no work in the hot sun for this child." He climbed up the steps leading to the front verandah, threw his *topee* and came into a corner and selecting a Singapore cane chair, made himself comfortable. The "boy" brought out tea and other drinks and left them on the table, and placing the soda-water under the table, carefully balanced the opener on top of one of them.

Evidently Long John understood what was said and began pouring out the tea. He asked me if I wanted something, but I was engaged watching a Santal funeral passing the house towards the *Sal* jungle, a man walking in front was scattering rice to left and to right. The funeral had also attracted the young gardener, who turning to Long John asked what the rice-scattering meant.

"These be jungle people and have strange manners and customs we know nothing of." Meanwhile the funeral had crossed the Government road and entered the *Sal* forest.

Ten minutes after, the *Chota Saheb*, as he was familiarly termed, for I had none to help me, got astride his stud and galloped off towards his own garden, two miles to the north to issue orders for the following day's work.

An hour after, the sun dipped behind the Nepal hills and shortly after, the disc of a brilliant full moon could be distinguished through the foliage of the *Sal* forest. A breeze had sprung up— a breeze welcome by all. Everyone seemed to take an interest in life again.

The hours dragged on, seven o'clock had given place to eight o'clock when Long John stepped out to announce dinner. Not to disappoint him I went in, sat down and played with my food. In spite of the breeze, it was really too hot to eat.

The bright moon had topped the trees while I dined, and on stepping into the verandah, I found the whole country bathed in its brilliant light. The silent coolie lines had become animated and from all sides the sound of Santal fiddles and flutes and the sound of the *Nagpuri* drums could be heard as they accompanied the songs of the dancers.

Beyond the northern coolie lines, on an abandoned tea estate. facetiously named *Awl*, a term signifying, "the deadly malarial fever," singing, dancing and drumming was being carried on with greater vigour. I had been informed that in a solitary hut a little inland from the left bank of the stream running through the estate, a marriage was to take place. The rice-beer usually supplied at all marriages on the tea garden had been copiously partaken of, hence the drumming and singing rising above all others.

Nine o'clock struck on a distant gong. Tired of sitting idle in the verandah, I went inside to finish a sketch. I soon found the centre room where I usually worked was a veritable oven. Throwing open every door and window I sat down to the drawing I had in hand; five minutes after I gave it up perspiring profusely. There was a make-shift *punkah* in the adjoining bed room, I went inside, undressed and went to bed, and was soon fast asleep. A ghastly sound, resembling nothing on earth, rent the air. I jumped out of bed wondering if I had heard it in my dream. Another and yet another unearthly shriek rent the stillness. I could not place the sound at all. I hastily donned some clothes, loaded every rifle and gun I had, and lit every lamp in the bungalow. The punkah had long ceased to function, the reason was obvious. Seizing the guns, I carried them into the small dining-room on the north side of the bungalow; for it was from this direction the sound had come. It was midnight by the clock. Peering through the window panes, which I had hastily closed, I tried to find some reason for the ghastly sound. Every coolie hut was barred, every line as silent as night, not even the dogs attempted to give vent to their feelings. From beyond the northern lines again that ghastly shriek pierced the stillness. Chaos now reigned. The Chinamen Carpenters, who lived fifty yards to the south of my abode, on the fringe of the *Sal* forest, frightened out of their wits, had collected all waste timber and pouring half a tin of kerosene oil on it had set it alight. Another man inside their house, suddenly blessed with a brain wave, set a Chinese record on their gramophone and started it going. Where peace had reigned, the beat of drums, the lighting of flares, the beating of anything that could make a noise, accompanied the shrieks of a frightened woman.

There was a knock on the door leading into the back verandah and an unrecognisable voice prayed to be let in. I opened the door hurriedly to find Long John, shivering with fright. He hurried inside, barred the door, and collapsed in a corner, calling on *Allah*.

Again that awful sound came to us louder than the din created by frightened coolies. It sounded nearer. Grasping a rifle, I went to the window to have a shot.

"*Huzoor*, don't fire, lest it come here and wreck the bungalow." Pleaded Long John.

"What is it? Come, let me know quickly."

"*Huzoor*, it is the *pagla hati*—a mad elephant. Some say, *huzoor*, it is *Saitan* himself."

"*Saitan* or no *Saitan*, make me a cup of tea."

Again that blood-curdling shriek broke the stillness of the night. Regardless of Long John's advice, I fired in the direction of the noise and waited. Evidently the shot had either killed or had frightened the beast, for as the minutes went by, the flares died down, the drumming and the hubbub ceased, and a silence fraught with fright settled down on the estate.

I went out into my front verandah with the cup of tea in my hand and was greeted by Achong, the head Chinaman, with these words:

"Your nursery gone to hell."

"What John?"

"Do tho' tha" (There were two.)

"Humra ghar tor dia." (They have broken my house.)

"Alright, John."

'Alright, going," and John went off.

Half an hour went by. The dawn was breaking. The coolies having recovered from their fright, were talking excitedly. I lit a cigarette, shouted for more tea and when Long John brought it, I found he too was his normal self again.

"Here, Long John, what has happened? What does Achong, Chinaman, mean by saying 'there were two'?"

"Huzoor, when that *pagla hati* shrieked, there were two wild elephants wandering in the *Sal* forest. These took fright and in running past the Chinaman's house, knocked their cook-room over. I was with the Chinaman at the time and saw them cross the stream, run through your *gotibari* (nursery) and disappear towards the Mechi river." Saying which he went inside.

"I wonder what damage has been done? Well, we can tell in the morning," I murmured to myself.

Gradually the light strengthened and as the burning orb appeared over the Dalka Forest and lit the tops of the near *Sal* trees, the *jungli murghis* hailed the appearance with crow after crow. A solitary figure from the nearest coolie lines crept towards my bungalow and reaching the steps, gazed up at me mutely, with frightened eyes.

It was *Sani Sirdar*, head of the *Kharia* coolies.

"What is it, *Sani?*"

There was no answer. Fright had effectually sealed his lips. I knew the remedy in cases of this sort. Shouting to Long John, I ordered him to bring the whisky bottle. When he brought it, I poured out a stiff peg and handing it to him, told him to give it to *Sani*.

"Well, *Sani?*" I asked as the last drop vanished down his throat.

"*Huzoor*, a terrible thing has happened."

"What thing?"

"*Huzoor*, I cannot speak even of it. Come and see."

Other sirdars had joined him.

"Alright. I'll be with you in five minutes." I went inside, hastily donned a coat and taking my *topee* from the verandah peg, went down the steps.

I followed the sirdars who led me past *Sani Sirdar's* lines, where several women were standing in a group. I chaffed them, but there was no answer. Poor creatures, I thought, they seem dumb with fright.

The sirdars walked on. We passed the northern lines and came to the hut where the marriage had taken place. It had fallen to the ground.

"Hullo, this was standing yesterday, how did it fall?"

Mangra Sirdar spoke. "*Huzoor*, as you know there was a marriage held here yesterday. While it was in progress, that *bhut* of a *hati* came up unawares. Even our line dogs were silent and none knew of his approach. We conclude he walked up the stream and up to this hut, which he put his head against and began shoving. As soon as the timber began to break, the men rushed out and seeing the elephant standing at the back of the hut, they lost their heads and ran away, leaving the women and children inside.

"I and Somra, had gone a little way when we stopped and came back. We were too late. As soon as the house began to fall, the *hati* came to the front and as the women rushed out one by one he caught them in his trunk and dashed them on the ground. We shouted to them to remain where they were. It was useless. The hut already on a bad slant was slowly, but surely coming down. The brute stood ready, he spared no one. Somra and I lifted one side of the hut, after the elephant had gone, and have put all the bodies inside. Come and see."

I went with him. The sight was heart-rending. The brute had done his work thoroughly and in sheer delight at the destruction emitted those horrible sounds we had heard in the night. I returned home dumbfounded. The *Chota hazri* laid out on the table I sent away untasted. I poured out a small glass of brandy and drank it down.

Seizing a telegraph form, I wired to the Magistrate to come over; instead, he had the elephant proscribed, offering a reward of Rs 250 to anyone who would kill it. Many of us have tried, not for the reward, but for the sake of the killing. Five of my bullets are embedded in him and others too claim to have hit him often. The animal seems to bear a charmed life. Five years ago the total number of human lives he had accounted for reached 135 and he still lives.

I heard his life history from a Nepalese crafter who lives in the Morung or Nepal Tarai. For years he wandered with a herd, the favourite of their leader, a fine female elephant. "One day", said Dalbir, "another young male, sought her favours challenging this one to an open combat. The fight took place in a large clearing in the forest lying between the Chalsa and Jaldakka rivers." "It was a very fierce fight, *huzoor*," continued Dalbir, "and the *pagla hati*, as he is now known, broke his right tusk. If you have watched him walking, he limps. The tusk of the younger elephant was buried below the joint. He left the herd disgraced, and, as if the cause of his downfall was due to mankind alone, he takes his revenge yearly on many human lives."

(1929)

Hunting With A Camera

By F.W. Champion

On the left bank of the Ganges, a few miles below Lachmanjhula, in the United Provinces, where the holy river emerged from the Himalayan foot-hills, lies a great forest which forms the home of many wild beasts from the mighty elephant and tiger downwards. Hardwar, that sacred and populous Hindu city, is only a few miles away on the other side of the river, and the pious pilgrims who come from all over India to wash away their sins by bathing in the holy water little realise how often at night tigers stand on the opposite bank of the river to watch with curious gaze the bright illuminations of their festivals, or how these huge beasts even listen to the rumbling of the trains as they bring the pilgrims to the railway station after long journeys from all parts of India.

In this forest for many years has resided a very fine tigress, who has so far escaped destruction at the hands of the numerous sportsmen who are for ever pursuing her—and may she continue to do so until old age mars her pleasure in the life which is as dear to her as their own is to her hunters! She is very powerfully built for a tigress and is perhaps as fine an example of her race as is to be found anywhere in northern India. For this reason the hunter who at last lays her low will undoubtedly feel very pleased with himself, although there are some amongst us—an increasing number these days, one is glad to be able to say—who can derive just as much pleasure from hunting with the bloodless camera, which, after all, takes no life and is much less selfish than shooting to kill, in that the resultant pictures can subsequently give pleasure to others in a way that skins or horns can never do even though the skin be stolen from one of the finest tigresses in northern India.

I will now describe a few episodes which have occurred from time to time during the last four or five years when we happened to be camping within this tigress' domain and have thus had opportunities to hunt her with a camera. The first time we became acquainted with her was several years ago, when she suddenly took to killing the buffloes which the local bamboo-cutters use for dragging their produce down to the edge of the Ganges, where the bamboos are tied together into huge rafts and floated away to distant markets on the banks of the great Ganges canals—those fine monuments of the work of the Irrigation Department in Upper India. During a single week she killed four or five of these buffaloes and always left the carcases to be devoured by vultures after making one heavy meal. Several times, mounted on a tame elephant, we searched the places where we hoped she would be lying up during the day, but she was never there and it appeared that there were two reasons for this. Firstly, she had at the time two or three small cubs to feed, which meant that she had to kill more frequently than usual, whereas an attack of rinderpest had greatly reduced the numbers of the sambar which form her usual food; and, secondly, she had been fired at in a beat and missed, so that she had learnt not to lie near her kills in the daytime. The result was that several natural kills produced no single glimpse of her to enable us to take a photograph, although one day a fine chital stag with his horns in velvet allowed us to approach within a few yards and seemed little perturbed at the click of the shutter as we recorded his picture. His very presence there, however, was a fairly certain indication that the tigress was not where we were hoping to find her. On another occasion, having once more failed to find our quarry, we followed a poor specimen of a sambar stag for two or three hours in the hope that he would stand in a good light and give us an opportunity to take his photograph; but he always moved too quickly from one belt of thick shade to another and all we could do was to snap him standing half-hidden among some bushes. Oh! If only the animal-photographer could explain to wild animals that, were they to stand out in the open for a few moments in a good pose, he would take their photographs, give them an honoured place on his wall or in his collection of jungle pictures and let them depart in peace!

But we are wandering from the subject of our tigress and must return. As we have already seen, she never seemed to be near her kills in the day-time, and, as she generally left them in the open, they were usually devoured by jackals and vultures long before the evening. She soon gave up killing the dragging cattle, which was as well for her, because, although the loss of these cattle was largely due to the carelessness of their owners, who calmly left them loose at night in places which they knew the tigress might visit, I should otherwise have had to make an effort to destroy her in the interests of my forest employees. We then tried tying up young buffalo-baits in very quiet secluded spots; but we soon found that the only places where she would kill these baits were open cross-roads, which meant that hyenas and jackals—which frequent jungle roads—always smelt them out and fired off the automatic flashlight arranged over the kills early in the evening and long before there was any hope of the tigress arriving. One day she killed a bait in a particularly quiet spot, and, full of hope, we mounted on a tame elephant and stalked the kill very quietly in the heat of the afternoon. Sure enough, we found her at last dozing in the shade of a bamboo clump and thus obtained our first view of her magnificent proportions. But she was evidently sleeping with one eye open, for, although there was ample time for a quick shot with a rifle, she dashed off with an angry "whoof" just as I was getting her into focus on the mirror of my reflex camera, so that once more she got the better of us. This particular kill, however, did not fail altogether as one of her cubs, who was by now three-parts grown, returned during the night and was caught by our automatic flashlight in the act of seizing the kill.

The next stage in our efforts to secure her photograph involved sitting out all night over a live-bait tied near an old kill, which we hoped would attract her to the spot and perhaps induce her to attack the living bait, over which the flashlight apparatus had been arranged during the day time so that it could be fired by pulling a cord from the machan. The reader will now accompany me in thought to this machan and in imagination spend the night with me in the tree. We will assume that the difficult adjustments of the flashlight apparatus have already been done—they take several hours and we are now mounted on a tame elephant and approaching the chosen spot at about 4 p.m. on a fine warm afternoon. As we draw near the place, we move very slowly and approach carefully under cover, since tigers in general and this tigress in particular have a habit of doing the unexpected and who knows but that we may now find her calmly eating her kill in broad daylight. But no: she is not here at the moment. A short distance from the old kill stands a dead tree on which are perched a number of vultures, evidently resting after their disgusting meal of putrid flesh, and above in the crystal clear sky, is circling a kite, also attracted by the prospect of food. We pause for a moment to watch the wonderful grace of the movements of his forked tail, which is a hundred-fold more efficient than the rudder of any ship or aeroplane invented by man, and then we move on again, noting as we approach the stealthy retreat of a pair of jackals, who have been stealing a meal during the absence of the rightful owner of the kill. We now climb up to the machan and, sending the elephant back to camp, settle down to the prospect of the deep enjoyment of a moonlight night spent absolutely alone in the heart of a great forest. All around us is a vast jungle containing no human being for miles in any direction, yet positively alive with wild animals and birds of every kind and description. Only a day or two previously a herd of about 20 wild elephants, including two or three tiny babies, passed under the very tree in which we are now sitting, and the place is notorious for sloth-bears, which come from long distances to feed on the luscious crop of berries now ripening on the *ber* bushes all around us. The local sambar have been sadly thinned out by a recent attack of rinderpest, but chital are common in the neighbourhood, which, among many other species, even holds a few of those curious four-horned antelope nowhere common in the Himalayan foot-hills. And the birds! Who can give any idea of the marvellous beauty and variety of the feathered denizens of the foot-hill forests? All around us are scores of peafowl, attracted like the bears by the ripening of the jungle fruits; green paroquets in hundreds are dashing about at a tremendous pace in every direction and screaming with joy in harsh raucous tones as through they are revelling in the thrill of their rapid motion through the air; bulbuls are twittering on almost every bush; plover of two or three species are running about the dry sandy *rau* bed in front of us; two or three kites are screaming in the air above us; a pair of fantailed flycatchers are pirouetting from twig to twig of the very tree in which we are sitting; and a host of others of every conceivable shape and colours are to be seen and heard in the directions. All seem bubbling over with a happiness which finds ready expression in song and play. And yet some naturalists claim that all Nature is intensely cruel! Those of us, however, who enjoy watching rather than destroying wild creatures do not find Nature cruel—far from it. Sudden death appears at intervals, it is true, but it is only our vivid imagination and fear of the hereafter that make us afraid of death. Wild creatures do not know what death is and are not troubled by thoughts about Heaven and Hell, so that the sudden passing of one of their number as the result of the advent of some flesh-eating animal or bird is but a fleeting incident soon forgotten by the survivors. But once again we are straying from our subject.

We sit happily on in our machan, hoping against hope that at last the tigress will give us our chance to take her photograph and imperceptibly the day passes away to be replaced by the full glory of a jungle night. Once or twice we hear the alarm cry of a kakar or chital in the distance and hope surges up in our hearts, only to die down again as the cries soon cease. Then a curious rumbling comes from the direction of Hardwar, some distance away, and we wonder what *tamasha* there can be making such a disturbance. But the noise seems to be increasing, and, at last, straining over the edge of the machan, we realise with dismay that a heavy storm is rapidly approaching from the west. What are we to do? We have no mackintosh and little bedding and our camp is several miles away, with a jungle full of. wild beasts in between and no lamp or path to help us get there. Yet if we stay in the *machan* we are bound to get wet through and thoroughly chilled, which will inevitably result in a bout of fever. Even as we consider the problem the moon disappears, dazzling lightning flashes across the sky in all directions, a strong wind begins to blow, and down comes a tropical deluge of rain which soon soaks the camera, flashlight, blankets, and finally us. All hope of our long-sought picture has gone, and, feeling distinctly nervous of being struck by lighting, we see in imagination our tigress hugging herself with glee at the thought of how well we are being punished for having had the impertinence to continue for so long in the vain pursuit of her photograph. At long last, after we have become resigned to spending a night of misery, we hear a curious whistling which does not seem to come from any animal or bird we recognise. Surely we are not beginning to get a little light in the head as a result of our nerve-racking experience? No: the whistling continues and increases in volume so that at last we realise, with a thrill of joy, that it must be one of our tame elephants, which, despite our orders to the contrary, has been sent out by my wife to rescue us from our predicament. We eagerly call up the elephant, thankful to escape from our chilly damp perch, and rapidly return to our comfortable camp 4 miles away, which we reach about 1 a.m. Shortly afterwards, fortified by hot Bovril, we are dozing in a comfortable warm bed and dreaming of new schemes for obtaining the photograph which had now become a fetish with us.

Thus the campaign continued for some years, but always without success. We could never find her again by stalking in the day-time; she always seemed to discover our presence if we sat in machans over her kills at night; and, if we arranged our automatic flashlight apparatus over her kills, she waited until hyenas and jackals had spent some time there first and thus fired the flashlight before she was due to appear. It seemed as though she were going to win in this contest of wits, and then, at last, we had a brilliant idea. We had a kill one day on the edge of a broad *rau* bed and we had noticed previously, from a study of her tracks, that she had formed the habit of hugging the foot of a low bank on the edge of this *rau* bed when passing this particular locality. How would it be if we were to arrange a tripwire at the edge of this bank, some distance from the kill, and thus avoid the risk of the chance being ruined by the inevitable jackals and hyenas? There seemed some hope of this method proving successful, especially as we had a good idea of the direction from which she was likely to arrive and could thus probably guide her, all unconsciously, by means of a judicious arrangement of cut branches, to the exact spot where our photographic trap was to be set. We decided to carry out this plan and arranged our apparatus with extreme care, even to the last detail of a trip-wire carefully matched to the colour of the surrounding ground for she had seen one of our trip-wires once before and carefully stepped over it without touching it! We then returned to our camp with a sneaking hope that at long last we stood a fair chance of winning in the long-drawn-out battle of wits. About midnight we heard the familiar boom of the exploding flashlight and we were so excited that we jumped out of bed and hurried out to the spot by the light of a lantern. Had we really succeeded at last, or had those ... hyenas and jackals once more ruined a good chance? After what seemed a tremendous time, although in reality the distance was quite short, we at last reached the spot and—hurrah! There were the tell-tale claw marks in the gound as she had involuntarily extended her claws on being startled by the noise and light of the exploding flashlight. Yes: the complicated mechanism of tripping the shutter had also worked without a hitch—it does not always do so—and at last our plate had been exposed. Now for the final stage of development. We rushed back to our camp, and, although it was the middle of the night, out came the developing chemicals, and before many minutes had passed we had the tremendous satisfaction of seeing a fine negative appearing in the developing dish—a negative which, except for a slight fault in one of the fore-legs, is as good as we had ever hoped to obtain even in our most optimistic moments.

Thus ended the hunt for the first negative of this fine tigress, to whom we take off our hats with heartfelt thanks for having given us such a fine run for our money. We could have shot her years before when we first saw her, and, had we done so, all would have been over except for a skin which would have begun rotting away by now under the effects of this trying climate. Yet she lives on and may still provide us with more harmless pleasure, so who can now say that, once we have overcome our primitive and savage lust of killing, hunting with a camera is not the peer of any form of blood-hunting that the world can produce.

(1929)

Drought in the Jungle

By F.W. Champion

"Of sapphire are the skies, but when men cry Famished, no drops they give."

LIGHT OF ASIA

Noon has passed some hours ago and the heat is now reaching its dreadful climax in the middle of the afternoon. A dull haze envelopes the whole jungle and the surrounding hills are but vaguely outlined against the sky, which, as though feeling in disgrace for having failed to produce one single drop of rain for a period of months, has now turned a dirty yellow colour—sullen and menacing. The previous monsoon has been a failure; the winter rains, which might have helped so much, were a bitter disappointment; the hot weather storms—the last hope—are still awaited. The inevitable result of such a shortage of the life-giving rain is that drought, cholera and famine, that dread trio, are now stalking forth, arm in arm, to take their fearful toll from man and beast, bird and fish, tree and plant alike. The trees have already dropped most of their leaves, in their valiant effort to save their lives by stopping transpiration of the little moisture which their far-spreading roots can suck up from the parched ground. The green grass, which should have sprung up after the winter-burning of the low-lying grassy areas, has completely failed and the hordes of half-famished cattle and herbivorous jungle animals are wandering aimlessly from place to place in their forlorn search for the food which practically does not exist.

The cattle, many of which have been brought from the famine-stricken village lands on the edge of the forest, form a terrible picture. Every rib stands sharply out from the tightly-drawn discoloured skin, the quarters are deeply sunken, the eyes staring, and many a miserable beast already carries the unmistakable hallmark of approaching death on its drawn and haggard face. The wild animals' plight, though bad, is perhaps not quite so serious as in the case of the cattle, for Nature's wild creatures are at all times far healthier and stronger than the domestic animals of man. Also, a denizen of the wilds, born and bred in the jungle, has much more experience in obtaining food when food is scarce than the miserable overworked and under-fed cattle of the Indian villager. The scavenging and carnivorous animals, on the other hand, although also put to trouble over the scarcity of water, are now waxing fat on the trials of their neighbours, just as the war profiteer grows bloated at the expense of his country and countrymen during times of stress. The tigers and leopards have little trouble in obtaining more food than they can eat, for the deer and cattle are too weak to look after themselves properly and are forced to drink at one or other of the very few remaining pools of water, even though they know that death in feline form is probably awaiting them there. As for the hyenas, foul but necessary scavengers that they are, they now feel that 'Der tag' has indeed come at last for them, and their hideous forms are to be seen everywhere each evening as they set out on their nightly bouts of gluttony. Even the very expression of their faces seems to have changed, if one may judge by the leering grin of one which passed near the camp the previous night—a grin which seemed to say "Ah: now it is my turn. I, the despised outcast, am coming into my own at last!"

The birds, also, except again those that prey on their lesser neighbours, are not their usual bright and happy selves. Many are now sitting about dejectedly in the stifling heat, with their beaks wide open in the vain effort to lessen the dryness of their throats. Here a crow, that impertinent and ubiquitous villain of the East, squats with his head thrown back and mouth gaping open, like an Indian sepoy waiting to receive his dose of liquid quinine on a sick-parade. There a magpie-robin, which, at this season of the year, usually sings happily to his mate as she sits comfortably on her nest in a neighbouring tree. True: following Nature's imperious call to reproduce their species, the nest is there and the faithful housewife is doing her duty nobly; but the insects which make up their food have nearly all died in the drought, and, unless the long-delayed rain should come in time, the two parents will be very hard put to find sufficient nourishment for the four or five voracious youngsters which will presently occupy the nest and clamour for food from morning till night.

Not far from the magpie-robin's nest and at the mouth of a gorge leading into the foot-hills, simmers in the heat a timber camp, where the contractors who are working within this area have collected their produce preparatory to taking it away in bullock carts to the nearest railway station some 25 miles away. Sawn scantlings and sleepers of pine and sal, toon and laurel-wood, are scattered about all over the place, while here and there men and dragging-buffaloes are lying down and making the most of what little shelter they can find from the scorching rays of the afternoon sun.

A deep hush lies over all, and the only sound to be heard is the creaking of the punkah in the forest rest house at the edge of the *parao*. Even this sound is not continuous, for the punkah sways but erratically to and fro in response to the dreamy efforts of the punkah-puller, who naturally feels that it is indeed hard that he alone should have to work while everyone else is resting. A short distance in front of the rest-house is a small pool of water, where the little hill-stream, one of the very few that have not yet dried up, makes its last appearance before disappearing under ground to be lost in the enormous bed of boulders, which, for untold ages, have rolled down the hills and now compose the bone-dry sub-soil formation of the bhabar tract. It is this pool of water that makes the place still habitable for man and beast and bird, and continuously all day and all night, a constant stream of thirsty creatures appears from all directions to drink of the life-giving fluid. At the moment the men and domestic animals are all dosing and the turn of the birds and more daring wild animals has come. A large party of langoors, seemingly quite indifferent to the blazing sun, are sitting about in the stoney stream-bed, and one or two are bending down in a most ungainly manner to lap up the tepid water, which has been stewing in the sun all day long. A jackal, fat and lazy as the result of the gargantuan feasts he has had during the last few weeks, is just sneaking back to the fetid carcase of a bullock which died of famine a few days ago. In a tree above the pool is a party of Paradise-flycatchers and what a vivid contrast there is between the almost unearthly beauty of the cock bird, with his snowy white livery, black crest, and long white tail, and the filthy sneaking appearance of the disappearing jackal! Surely one might mistake the one for a wanderer from Heaven and the other as one of Satan's minions, waxing fat on the present troubles of other creatures. If this were truly the case, the former would certainly find the Earth, in its present famine-stricken and sun-scorched state, a very poor substitute for the lush gardens of Paradise.

Presently a stir arises among the drowsy human beings in the camp, for word passes round that a *musth* wild elephant, driven almost mad by a combination of his temporary functional derangement and the lack of sufficient water, is advancing through the jungle towards the pool and must pass right through the stacks of timber to reach his objective. A *musth* elephant is a creature that is treated at all times with the greatest respect by everyone, from the mighty tiger downwards, and a *musth* elephant that is also suffering from heat and thirst may only too easily become a murderer on the slightest provocation. Once the dread news is out there comes a sudden stampede, as everyone flees to leave the thirst-racked creature a clear path to the water which he must and will have, for he, a lover of the night and the cool depths of the jungle, must be in desperate straits indeed to have ventured out in the open blazing sun in the middle of such an afternoon. Then once more the hush falls—this time a hush pregnant with the possibility of coming events. Even so, one or two of the human inhabitants of the *parao*, more daring than their fellows, hide themselves among the bushes on the line of approach of the elephant and nervously wait to watch his arrival.

For a short time absolute silence reigns; then comes a cracking of dry leaves and branches. Once again all is still and it seems that he must have stopped. But no: he suddenly comes into view and—what a splendid sight he is. A magnificent *makna*, fully 10 feet in height at the shoulder, striding slowly along with stately majestic tread, he looks the veritable giant among wild elephants that he really is. His head is held very high, he appears to tower among the neighbouring trees, and his whole appearance is suggestive of utter contempt of any lesser creature that may dare to block his path. The dark *musth* discharge on his cheek is still clearly visible, but he is evidently nearing the end of his functional derangement; his whole body is drawn and emaciated, partly as a result of his musth state, and partly from lack of water and sufficient food; his eye is sunken and angry, and, although he is evidently not in a blood-thirsty mood, woe betide any creature that dares to check his progress. Thus he moves steadily forward and one wonders how many scores of years have passed over that stately head; how often has he seen the jungle stricken with drought and famine like the present; how many times has he visited this life-giving pool of water in similar circumstances?

By now he has reached the timber *parạo*, which may check his progress or cause his slumbering temper to arise. But no! He pauses not for a moment, nor does he deflect a yard to the right or left. Straight through the *parao* among the cut timber he advances, seemingly unconscious of the cowering workmen who are lying concealed here and there among the logs, and now at last he is within sight of the water which has drawn him here at this unusual hour. A man in similar circumstances would rush the last few yards and eagerly lap up the precious fluid, but this jungle monarch shows not the slightest sign of eagerness or excitement. On he goes at exactly the same pace, advancing like inexorable Fate, until at last he has reached the pool and his greatly needed drink and bath are at hand. Even now he does not hurry, but pushes the end of his trunk gently into the water, carefully washes out the trunk, and then, with one sharp intake of his breath, draws up two or three bucketfuls of the tepid liquid. He then lifts up his trunk to squirt the water over his heated body and one can feel with him the intense satisfaction that he obtains as the water trickles down his enormous flanks and washes away the dust and dirt which have collected on his body during his tiring journey to the pool. Again and again he draws up trunkfuls of water, sometimes squirting it right up in the air so that it falls over him like a shower-bath, sometimes shooting it right down into his soft fleshy mouth, and sometimes swishing it over those muscular legs which must have carried his great frame tens of thousands of miles during the century of more that he has spent in these forests. Once or twice he pushes the end of his trunk further than usual down his throat and then vibrates his body in a most astonishing manner as though he were trying to force the water to the very extremities of his parched and somewhat emaciated frame.

In the meantime the human refugees, realising at last that this elephant is far too absorbed in his enjoyment of the water to pay any attention to them, gradually creep nearer to watch the unusual scene. First one and then another of the jungle workmen and camp servants collect on the edge of the stream-bed some fifty yards away, until at last two score or more spectators are there, even including the Forest Officer's little four-year-old daughter, who, in her short life, has already had fine views of a tiger and a leopard, to which is now added the almost unique picture of a *musth* wild elephant bathing in broad daylight only a few yards distant from a forest-camp. The spectators finally lose all fear, and, squatting about quite openly all over the place, freely comment on the elephant's figure and manner of bathing, as though they were watching some performance in a circus. Yet, even now, although the human voice is usually anathema to a wild elephant, this monarch of the jungle pays not the slightest attention, but remains entirely absorbed in his own occupation. Perhaps he regards human beings with the contempt which many of them deserve and does not even notice their existence, or may be his mind and intelligence are befogged as the result of his affliction combined with the parching thirst which may have been racking his body for many days past.

In any case, he remains for perhaps fifteen minutes longer and then, satisfied at last, he turns, still not deigning even to glance in the direction of his audience, and strides off at exactly the same even steady pace that marked his arrival. As he leaves the open river-bed to reach the tree jungle, he passes over some soft sand, where he leaves clear foot-prints 5' 1" in circumference. Twice the circumference of an elephant's fore-foot gives the height at the shoulder almost to an inch, so that he thereby proves that, even though he has no tusks, he is over 10' in height, and, as regards size at any rate, fully deserves his claim—as testified by his magnificent appearance and bearing—to be a veritable monarch among the numerous denizens of these famous jungles.

(1929)

Shooting in the Doon

By John O'Lynn

Huzoor, anything may come out in this jungle," the local guide assured me. "As you can see, it is really a continuation of the Government Forest and you are only the second sahib who has had permission from the *zemindar* to shoot here this year. The first, a Major Sahib, should have shot a tiger but he was too intent on watching a *cheetal* which was approaching him and he did not see the tiger go by."

Promising, what? Miles and miles of *sal* forest rising gradually into the lower hills fringing the Western Doon wherein lay the reserved Government Forest. As I had never before shot in a submontane area I had not yet seen a tiger nor yet—curiously enough—even a sambhur or *cheetal* in the wilds, though I had, at various times, shot two panther and two bear in the Hills. The present prospect of "anything at all" was distinctly pleasant.

The beaters—nearly a score in number—were arranged for and drawn into line with instructions from my guide as to the direction they should take. I was led away from them, through a maze of *sal*, and posted just over the crest of a knoll, behind a handy tree whence I obtained a fair view for nearly a hundred yards around.

My journey had been the best part of three-quarters of a mile but the beaters were, in a direct line, a matter of seven or eight hundred yards away.

They had started. Nearer and nearer came their shouts. Now they must be a mere three hundred yards distant. Still no cry, louder than usual, marking the advent of some large animal.

Suddenly from out of a small nullah in the labyrinth around me dashed a large *cheetal* stag. He paused a moment and though his head was then hidden behind two closely-growing trees I had seen enough to realise his was a head worth having. A second sufficed to bring my rifle to my shoulder, less than another for a quick aim at an easy shot at about sixty yards and.. .. ..the lovely creature fell like a log.

A rapid re-load—even before the stag lay on the ground—and, still crouched behind my tree, I awaited the beat. No, nothing more. The beaters began to emerge, I whistled up my companion and we met where the *cheetal* lay.

Confound! Still partly in hard velvet! What a nuisance to find my very first *cheetal* to be one I would not have shot had I properly seen his horns. *Hm!* All his own fault for putting his head where it was screened!

However, he was a full thirty-one inches and there was really very little velvet to peel off. "It *would* come off", said the crowd. Right, I would try not to regret my share in the tragedy, even though it was not wholly my fault, for *cheetal* were actually "open".

Back in triumph to the car where the luggage-carrier was given an unusual load. The first tragedy was over.

II

My orders were strict that the *cheetal* head be hung up in the sun every day to expedite the process, already started, of the velvet peeling. For three days, therefore, had the head hung from a nail, some six feet off the ground, in front of the *Dak* Bungalow where I was staying.

On the third afternoon I returned from my work, a couple of miles away, to find that consternation reigned in my camp. The head had remained unwatched for a short time because of the temporary absence of the watchman for the time being. These things *will* happen and it is a wise man who refrains from too close an inquisition but contents himself with a wholesome strafe all round!

"What dog was it?" was one of the few questions I allowed myself.

"*Huzoor*," volunteered a servant, "it must have been that black and white female dog of the *bania's*—the one whose shop is on the main road near the *serai*. I saw it prowling around here just before we discovered that the head had been pulled off the wall."

"Do you mean the one I saw with puppies playing around it the other day?" I asked.

"Yea, Huzoor, that very one—the mis-begotten wretch!" came the eager reply.

Once more—"*Confound!*" I gazed longingly at the ruined symmetry of my thirty-one inch (and *first*) *cheetal* head. No power on earth could now restore its lost beauty. Four clear inches had been gnawed off the right horn—just when it had begun to peel so splendidly too and I was on my way to having a trophy worth keeping.

However! I thought of the emaciated form of the mother-dog I had seen. Less than the proverbial bag-o'-bones, she was dependent chiefly on such scraps as were thrown to her for the existence of herself and four very jolly little pi-pups. ... Dash it all! How could I nurse wrath against her—even though I too had been the object of her frantic barks as I had passed by her master's shop. "Poor thing" was the unpractical thought which persisted in rising in my mind as I thought of both her unfailing care of her whelps and her apparently unending watch over the *bania's* shop. She had not merely to live; she had two very distinct jobs in life and I could not find it in me to be too hard about it.

"Very well," I ordered. "Orderly, you alone go and tell the *bania* not to allow his dog to come scavenging around here again. If she causes any further damage, however, tell him that I shall hold him responsible."

Even while compliance was assured I could see disappointment in some of the faces of my staff. I am sure that they would have loved an opportunity to have gone off and thrown their weight about a bit more possibly till the *bania* had, for peace's sake, sold them some flour at less than favourable rates!

There it was, the second tragedy. The head was ruined beyond recall but, because of some silly urge within me, I could forgive and try to forget. To forget wholly was impossible. Curious, eh?

III

Two afternoons later my shikari came to me with news which was always most welcome—a panther kill of the night before. Would I sit up? Yes, he had found the kill and, if I could come, he would make a machan. Time and distance were no obstacle as the place was a bare thirty yards from the main motor road. We went there and, after a brief look around, I decided to sit on the ground. The kill was a few paces down the bank of a shallow nullah and hidden under some very dense scrub. Above was a field of wheat. To the right was the road and to the left, circling below the field, was a dense scrub through which lay the panther's only way if he wanted—as of course all panthers want—cover on his way to his meal.

Some fifteen yards back, in the field, stood the only tree available for a machan; but it would have involved a long and very sketchy shot at a tangent, as it were, over the edge of the field. On the other hand, a large tree stump on the edge of the field provided a convenient base for a good bower on the ground and I decided to use it thus. Moreover, it was only some eighteen feet from the kill.

The shikari had certainly made a good job of it by the time I went back and I settled down in my "synthetic bush" at a quarter to seven. There was no need to get in earlier. A good deal of traffic passed along the road—bullock carts, men from fields near by, and even occasional motors. About a hundred yards away, on some open ground at the foot of the nullah, lay an encampment of picturesque men from far-off Bashahr State who had brought their herds of long-haired goats down into these foothills for winter grazing. These men moved about their evening tasks talking and singing without restraint while their very large and woolly dog bayed intermittently against the chafe of his chain. Life was altogether a noisome affair.

Patient and motionless did I sit, watching the sky change from blue to grey and then into that "faded" black, the herald of true night. Sounds of traffic grew more and more infrequent and by half-past seven I had begun to stay really vigilant. The moon had risen and, while it cast a brilliant band of light on about two-thirds of the distance between me and the kill, it failed to pierce the thicket over the kill. It became quite a game to try to see anything in there. I had to give it up after a time as I found I was unduly straining my eyes in the effort. I had, in consequence, to depend on my ears which I attuned to the silence around me to enable me to pick up any sound that arose.

How time can drag when one is sitting still! At eight-fifteen I heard a slight and distant purr.

"Hello! Spots coming?" I wondered.

Not a bit of it. My companion in the *Dak* Bungalow (as I learnt later) had returned unexpectedly from his inspections of roads and bridges, heard that I had gone out for a panther and came out to verify the information. Blighter! How I mentally swore at the glare of his headlights and the hum of his engine as he made his inquiries from my men on the road before he swung back again. This was the approaching purr which, for a few glad seconds, I had hoped was that of a cheerful big cat approaching his dinner.

When would I get my dinner that night? I had confidently laid down that I would sit till at least midnight because I quite agreed with the shikari that if the panther returned at all he would most probably come long after sunset. Now, however, as 9 p.m. drew near the heartening effects of a substantial tea were beginning to . . . er! . . . wear off! Nor could I tighten my belt—I was wearing braces!

That Bashahr dog, too, was beginning to annoy me. "*Whoof-whoof-whoof*" he kept on at the strange sounds of night which had now replaced the hush of late evening.

Would he never stop for more than ten seconds at a time? Could it be that the panther was about and that the dog had sensed its proximity? A wretched buffalo, tethered apparently somewhere below on my left, had now joined forces with the baying dog.

"*Ugh-h-h-h*" softly grunted the buffalo in the brief intervals that the dog allowed the silence I so much desired. "*Whoof-whoof-whoof*" gaily responded the dog!

My resolutions about midnight wavered. What was the use of so protracted a vigil? I would make it eleven o'clock and call it a night.

9-30 now and a deep hush prevailed—save for that infernal dog and the low grunts of the buffalo. Would I make it 11 or just 10-30—or perhaps even 10? Yes, perhaps 10 only!

9-45 and not a sign of the panther . . . . Stay! Surely that was the light crackle of a dry leaf below me? No. There were too many dry leaves about and a panther would make much more noise. It must be a jackal or a wild cat. Anyhow, I would look and furnish myself with a perfectly sound excuse for getting back, for if a jackal came on the kill it meant that the panther was not about and not likely to come for hours—if at all.

Taking the precaution to align my gun in the direction of the kill I pressed the button of my torch.

Heavens! The panther himself—above the kill and broadside on!

How his yellow fur with its dark rosettes gleamed in the brilliant light! I had time to notice how he strove in vain to peer into the flood of light which fell on him from fifteen feet.

In much less time than it takes to narrate I sighted and my finger curved lovingly around the trigger. The crash of my shot danced into a pandemonium which ensured for a few seconds.

"*Whoof! Wa-wa-wa-wa-wa!*" and the stricken animal tore through the undergrowth—forwards and down the *nallah*.

Silence. Then a flurry of leaves—his death-struggle, as we saw later, but which got me switching on my torch again in a fevered hurry lest he were coming up to investigate the cause of his downfall! Then complete silence—even on the part of the probably awed dog and the buffalo.

My men came from the road to my whistle, we gathered up my belongings and, giving the panther time to settle down to his last sleep, I went back to dinner.

Half an hour later I returned and with torches going and each step taken after a very cautious look around, we found the great cat already growing cold. He must have died immediately and so the distance he had travelled amazed me the more. The shot, moreover, seemed a good one.

I was interested to learn also that no buffalo had been in the neighbourhood that night and that I had been listening to Felis pardus himself swearing softly at the dog's incessant challenge.

The main question was lost sight of as we recognised the identity of the dog, confirmed on inquiry from the owner.

"Yes, *Huzoor*," said the *bania*, "as you know she was given to wandering a lot and I missed her in the morning. She must have run out at night at the panther and so been carried off. Oh, she was a very good chowkidar and I am sorry to lose her but we shall all bless you for ridding us of this pest, the panther."

Poor old mother pi-dog! She had, in death, given me a trophy far more handsome and more valued than even a first *cheetal* head. She had also, through my agency, encompassed the downfall of a public enemy.

She was now wholly and unequivocally forgiven because of this, her share in the completion of the cycle of jungle tragedies.

(1929)

Hunters of Souls

By Augustus Somerville

During a long period of service in the Survey Department of the Government of India, I have had occasion to visit many of the remotest parts of India, away from the beaten tracks and devoid of those forms and amenities of civilization that the average traveller learns to expect.

It was on one of these excursions that I came across an extraordinary tribe living in the heart of the mountain fastnesses of Chhota Nagpur. These people who call themselves Bhills, but who, I have reason to suspect from their colour, language and facial expressions, are closely related to the Sontal and Ghond tribes, are a nomadic, semi-barbaric race living exclusively on wild animals, in the snaring and trapping of which they are experts, and also on their reputation as "Soul Catchers." In this last extraordinary avocation I was most interested, but could glean no information from the natives themselves until one day I had an opportunity of watching a "Soul Catcher" at work.

Early in October 1908, I received orders to survey a large section of forest land in the Palamu District. Certain wise-acres had discovered traces of minerals, such as mica, coal, etc., in the neighbourhood and were making tentative offers for the purchase of a large tract of this land, with mining rights thrown in. A wide awake Government hearing that I had a mining engineer's certificate attached to the many credentials that secured me this position, decided to send me down to survey the land, and incidentally report on its possibilities as a mining area.

I will hasten over the first part of journey as uninteresting but once at Daltonganj, a small station on the extreme end of the only decent motoring road in the district, I found myself on the brink of the unknown.

Next morning I procured a hand-cart for the transport of my tent, guns, ammunition, etc., and with two servants and a native guide, set out for the interior.

The only road was a rough cart track, which after we had followed for about six miles, disappeared in the impenetrable undergrowth through which we were compelled to travel; abandoning the cart, we bundled the tent and accessories into three packs, which my two servants and the guide carried, and shouldering my rifle myself, set out on the 30-mile trek that would eventually bring us to the village of the Soul Catchers.

That night we camped on the edge of the jungle, near the banks of a small stream. In a short time we had the tent erected and a good fire blazing merrily. Dangerous animals were numerous in the district and after a good dinner I turned in, with my rifle fully loaded on the cot besides me.

Nothing untoward occurred that night, but in the early hours of the morning the servants awoke me with the disquieting information that our guide had disappeared.

Needless to say I took this information very seriously. To be without a guide in that wilderness of unchartered forest and impenetrable bush was alarming enough, but what worried me most was that I had supplies only for a couple of days, and the possibilities of locating the village without a guide was remote enough to depress the most sanguine of explorers.

I will never forget the three days we wandered in that forest. It was one of the most awful experiences I have ever had.

From the onset I had determined to travel light and so abandoned the tent and other heavy accessories. My survey instruments, I buried securely in the vicinity of a large *pepul* tree, marking the spot with several heavy boulders from the adjoining stream, then carrying only our food, guns and ammunition, set out for the nearest human habitation.

Directing myself solely with my pocket compass I travelled due south-east the direction we were taking prior to the guide's disappearance. Of beaten tracks there were none, but hitherto we had managed to avoid the worst sections of the forest fairly successfully. Bereft of the experience and woodcraft of our guide we blundered into all manner of pitfalls, and on several occasions found ourselves in thick masses of undergrowth composed almost entirely of stunted plum bushes fairly bristling with thorns, that tore our clothes and lacerated our hands and legs fearfully. All that day we trekked through a waterless section of the forest and suffered agonies from heat and thirst. Towards evening, however, we emerged on an open plain on the edge of a vast swamp. My two servants were advancing slightly ahead of me, and as they left the forest and saw the cold water ahead, they threw down their burdens and raced towards the marsh. At this instant I also broke from the entangling bushes on the edge of the swamp and all but followed their example, so parched was I, when I beheld a sight that for a moment kept me spellbound. As the natives reached the water-edge, two huge black forms rose, and with a snort of rage made for the unfortunate men. In a moment I had recognised the animals for the powerful fearless wild buffalo of the Chhota Nagpur plateau. Unslinging my rifle from my shoulder, I fired at the animal nearest to me but in my haste aimed too low, so that the bullet, intended for the shoulder, penetrating the animal's knee. The buffalo went down with a crash and as I turned to fire at its mate, I realised with a thrill of horror, that I was too late. The second unfortunate Indian in his haste to leave the water had slipped on the marshy banks and lay floundering in the mire. In a moment the buffalo was on him and with one mighty sweep of its huge horns hurled his body through the air to land a mangled mass of bones and flesh some ten feet from the bank. At this moment it spotted me, and with a snort of rage charged in my direction. I am afraid I let no sporting sentiments interfere with my shooting. Working the bolt of my rifle steadily from my shoulder—my rifle being of the magazine pattern—put four successive shots into the huge brue in as many seconds, so that it went down as if pollaxed.

By this time my remaining servant, trembling with the shock of his recent experience, had reached my side and reloading, I went towards the wounded buffalo. Although handicapped with its broken legs the animal was nevertheless, making a gallant effort to get out of the deep mire that hampered its movements. As we approached the beast, it glared at us and with a savage bellow attempted to charge. Awaiting till it had approached sufficiently close, one well-directed shot put an end to its miseries, and we were safe to attend to our unfortunate comrade.

Poor fellow, he must have been killed instantaneously; covering up the body with a piece of cloth, we dug a shallow grave and buried him as decently as possible. By this time it was getting dark, so we built a fire and camped a short distance away.

That night I slept badly. The excitement of the evening and the strangeness of the situation kept me continuously awake. Towards morning the cold became intense and unable to sleep, I determined to rise, replenish the fire and if possible boil some water for an early cup of tea.

Leaving the shelter of the bush in which I lay, I walked briskly towards the place where I had seen Mohamed Ali stock our small store of edibles. Unable to find them I was first under the impression that I had mistaken the spot, but a closer inspection showed a few remaining packages containing flour and sugar.

Shouting loudly to Mohamed Ali to wake up, I started a feverish search in the surrounding bushes for further signs of the stores but although I wandered far into the forest, not a single trace of food could I find. Incensed with Mohamed Ali for his carelessness and blaming myself bitterly for not carefully attending to the storing of this essential part of our equipment more carefully, I awaited the arrival of my servant impatiently determined to give him a bit of my mind.

I must have waited fully half an hour still searching round in the hope of finding part of the missing stores before I was aware that no Mohamed Ali had turned up.

"What on earth is the matter with the fellow", I wondered. "He surely cannot be still asleep."

Returning to the camp, I looked all round for him. His blanket lay in a ruffled heap on the spot where he had slept, but of the man himself there was no trace.

All that morning I waited, searching the surrounding forest and even firing my rifle occasionally in the hope of attracting his attention if the poor fellow had wandered into the forest and lost his direction, but to no avail and at last I was compelled to admit that henceforth I would have to travel alone.

Imagine my position. One of my servants killed, two mysteriously spirited away in the dead of night and no provision of any sort except a little flour and sugar to sustain me till I reached a human habitation of some type.

To say I was depressed, is to put it mildly. Candidly I was more than depressed, I was scared. The vision of myself parched with thirst, faint from starvation, wandering through the dense forest, a prey to any wild animal I chanced to meet, filled me with the gravest apprehensions.

Keep on I knew I had to. To stay where I was, would only diminish my chances of reaching civilisation, so that while I had the strength and ability I determined to push on depending on my good fortune to strike some village.

Cutting first a generous supply of meat from the carcass of one of the buffaloes, I had shot the evening previous, I packed the few things I needed and with as much ammunition as I could carry, set out on my lonely trek.

All that day I worked steadily south-east, but although I kept a sharp lookout, I failed to detect any signs of human habitation.

That night, fearing to sleep on the ground alone, I looked around for a convenient tree and after singeing a portion of the meat over a small fire, I ate a frugal meal, and climbed to the topmost branches.

The evening was still light and I scanned the forest in every direction. On every side was an unending vista of green and yellow leaves broken here and there by small clearings, but of villages no sign existed.

The night fell quickly, and soon a glorious moon sailed over the tree tops flooding the rustling, billowy sea of green below me, with a soft translucent light. It was a night, which in spite of my precarious position, I recall with the keenest delight.

Scarcely had the darkness fallen when a sambur belled in a thicket nearby and soon the forest awoke to its nocturnal life of mystery and movement.

From my lofty perch, I watched a herd of spotted deer troop past my tree, pursued by a stealthy yellow form which I instantly recognised for a huge leopard. I could have shot the beast easily, so unaware was he of any human presence, but I refrained from firing and later was thankful for this forbearance.

As the night wore on, I settled myself more comfortably in the deep fork of the tree and was soon asleep.

I may have slept a couple of hours, perhaps less, when I was awakened by a peculiar throbbing sound that seemed to fill the forest.

I roused myself and looking round eagerly soon detected the direction from which the sound was proceeding. As it approached, I recognised the low droaning of the large drums the Sontals in this district use and I must confess the thought of human beings filled me with a strange sensation of joy and relief.

Fortunately a natural prudence restrained me from springing from my perch and hastening in the direction of the drums. Waiting till the first of the drummers emerged from the thick forest I raised myself and was about to call out when I noticed that the leading natives, bearing huge flaming torches, were nude, except for a single loin cloth and grotesquely decorated in yellow and vermillion. The torch-bearers were followed by others hideously painted in white and black representing skeletons. These extraordinary beings were executing a wired type of dance and chanting a solemn dirge, while immediately behind them, slung from bamboo poles, were the bodies of two men. The vanguard of this strange procession was formed of a large crowd of Sontals armed with spears, bows and arrows and various other crude weapons.

The procession passed immediately under my tree and as the bearers of the two corpses, (as I took them to be) were beneath me, I looked down and received quite a shock—the bodies were those of our guide and my servant Mohamed Ali.

Waiting till the procession had passed, I took my rifle and slipping from the tree followed cautiously in their wake.

I had not far to go. Reaching a clearing, the procession stopped. As the dancers and musicians advanced, each threw his burning torch on the ground and in a little while there were a heap of torches burning fiercely, around which the whole procession gathered.

Concealing myself in the bushes a short distance out of the circle of light I watched in amazement the strange rites that now followed.

First of all the two bodies were laid side by side on the ground close to the fire. Two of the dancers more grotesquely decorated than the others and whom I rightly conjectured were high priests of this strange sect, advanced and raising each body in turn, set the pole into a hollow in the ground, so that the bodies now confronted the dancers in an upright position. The instant the firelight fell on their faces I realised with a thrill of horror that both men were alive, but so drugged or otherwise stupefied that they hung loosely in their fastenings swaying like drunken beings.

No sooner was this done, then the whole circle of dancers sprang into activity. Round and round the fire they whirled, chanting a queer plaintive refrain, punctuated with staccato beats from the muffled drums. For a long while they danced till at last weary with their exertions, they gave a final shout and settled down once more.

The two priests now advanced. Going up to the captives they raised their heads and forced them to drink some concoction which they poured from a pitcher brought by one of the dancers. Whatever the drink was, it must have been a powerful restorative. Within five minutes both men were fully awake and conscious of all that was taking place round them.

What, I wondered, would be the ultimate fate of these two men. It was not likely that in a district so near to British administration they would attempt a cold-blooded murder, but had I known what was to follow, death would have been a merciful release.

Seeing that both men were now perfectly conscious, one of the priests arose and taking a long sharp knife in his hands advanced towards his victims. I fingered my trigger uneasily, uncertain to fire or not, but determined at all cost to save the lives of those two servants of mine. Instead of injuring them, however, he commenced a long harangue. Pointing frequently towards the prisoners and then into the forest in the direction in which I had come, he seemed to be working his followers up to some momentous decision and he was not long in gaining their unanimous support. The moment he stopped, with one voice, the whole tribe chanted *"Maro, maro"* (Kill, kill) and, with a swiftness that completely deceived me, the priest struck twice, and the red blood gushed down the chests of the victims. Quickly I slung my rifle round, bringing the foresight to bear on the murderer. But from the moment of that one fierce shout and the anguished cry from the two prisoners, not a further sound could be heard. A strange tense expectant hush seemed to fill the forest. On the face of the two prisoners were depicted the most abject terror, their wounds, probably superficial, bled profusely, but the men were unaware of the blood, instead they stood staring before them into the forest waiting for some awful apparition to come,— and come it did.

Swiftly, silently, remorseless as death itself came a queer sinister shape. Not two feet high, semi-human in form, its hair, straggling and entangled all over its body, its face hideous, with two great eyes darting out of cavernous sockets, it leapt and gambolled out of the forest, into the clearing and with a shrill maniacal laugh stood confronting the two prisoners.

So hideous, so repulsive was this awful creature, that my rifle forgotten I stood staring, unable to believe my eyes; and then started a dance the likes of which I have never seen.

Whirling slowly at first, advancing, retreating, this grotesque human shape, fluttered up and down before the terror-stricken silent men. Gradually the pace increased, a drum. commenced to throb gently, swifter grew the dance and swifter, louder grew the drums and louder the chanting of the priests joined the roll of the drums, slowly, one by one, the other dancers joined in, the spectators swayed by a common impulse beat time to the ever swelling music, and the prisoners, hypnotised by the rhythm of sound and movement round them, sank lower and lower, till they hung inert, their bonds alone supporting them.

The end came suddenly, dramatically. A rifle shot rang out a sharp command, and a thin line of khaki-clad figures broke from the cover of the jungle and surrounded the dancers.

In a moment pandemonium broke loose. Surprised, startled and wholly unprepared, the dancers and priests broke and fled for the cover of the surrounding forests. Anxious to join the melee I broke from the cover of the forest and rushed towards the fire. At that instant I came face to face with one of the presiding priest.

With a fine disregard for sacerdotal procedure, I jammed my rifle butt into his ribs that he went down with a groan and stayed there. Reaching my two servants, I hastened to undo their bonds, and while engaged in this task was suddenly seized from behind and swinging round found myself face to face with a young Police Officer.

"Well I'm damned. If it isn't the very man we are looking for," he cried with surprise. "What on earth are you doing here?"

"Can't you see," I said, "Getting these two poor devils out of the scrape they have got into."

Mutual explanation followed and I learned that from the moment I had left Daltonganj I had been shadowed by members of this tribe under the mistaken impression that I was an Excise Officer on one of my periodical raids into the interior. The guide had been overpowered and carried off the first night in the hope that without a guide further progress would be impossible, but as I continued, all unknown to me, in the right direction, my servant Mohamed Ali suffered the same fate.

Anxious to avenge themselves on what they considered were informers of the Police, these two men were taken into the heart of the forest and handed over to the "Soul Catchers". The rites I witnessed were explained to me by the young Police Officer who had arrived on the scene so opportunely.

The men were first drugged with a native concoction containing *bhang*. On arrival at the scene of operations, they were given an antidote and restorative, and later branded in the chest by the priests, so that they were marked men for life. Next a strange half-demented creature, who lived in that part of the forest and who was credited with supernatural powers, danced before the victims who were thus hypnotised and in this condition made to believe that their souls had left them and were in the keeping of the "Soul Catchers." They were seldom harmed physically, but were socially ostracised, driven from village to village and refused even the ordinary necessities of life. The hardships of such an existence usually drove these poor creature crazy or they died from starvation and neglect. None dared to assist them for fear of incurring the enmity of the "Soul Catchers" themselves. There was, however, a method of release and many took this course. By selling all they possessed, they would raise the necessary amount of money needed and this on being paid to the high priest of the sect, a ceremony was performed by which the unfortunate victim regained his soul and his position in society. Although in the turmoil that followed the first rush of the Police, the strange creature I had seen, eluded the troops and disappeared in the forest, the high priest of the sect I had knocked senseless with my rifle, was secured and duly appeared in Court. I will never forget the sensation he created, when in his full regalia he appeared in the dock to answer the charges against him. Although I formed the principal witness, he produced an alibi that was unshakable— in fact the whole village turned out *en masse* prepared to swear that on that particular night this self-same priest was asleep in his hut in the middle of the village and that the whole case was a Police plot brought up out of spite.

He was eventually convicted and got three years hard and the tribe of "Soul Catchers" shifted to healthier quarters, but to this day I never visit Daltonganj and the neighbouring villages without a strange sensation of being watched and spied on.

(1932)

Encounters With Big Game

By 'Surfield'

The remark has often been made to me, "You survey people must get wonderful opportunities for big game shooting."

Actually this is by no means the case. Big game shooting takes time; and the survey officer who is here today and gone tomorrow, has not the time to spare to follow up news of big game in his vicinity. He must hasten on to see the work of his next surveyor. It is inevitable, however, if one tours for months on end in the jungle, to have some encounters with big game; and such encounters are no less exciting for being unexpected.

Wild elephants are common in many parts of Burma, and for long after my first arrival in the country, I was anxious to see something of them. For hundreds of miles I walked or rode through good elephant country without encountering one. Fresh tracks were frequently in evidence, but always the elephants had moved on a short time before and were nowhere to be seen. After a time I ceased to expect to see one. Then, as it so often does in the jungle, the unexpected happened.

I was testing the work of a surveyor, and in company with his squad, we were walking along a level and fairly good jungle trail in single file. I led, closely followed by the surveyor, and the squad was a few yards behind. A crackling from a clump of bamboos a few yards away made me pause.

"Is that an elephant?"

"No, sahib, only monkeys," was the reply; and we went on.

A few yards further on I caught sight of an object, about thirty-five yards from the path, which at first glance I took to be a large boulder. A second glance however showed it to be a solitary bull elephant slightly turned away, and apparently unconscious of our presence. I expected it to make off as soon as it heard us, but as we had no gun with the party it seemed just as well to try to slip by quietly and not disturb it. Before I could motion to those behind to be quiet, however, there was a loud exclamation from one of the Indian *khalasis*,

"*Hathi!*"

The sequel was as instantaneous as unexpected. The elephant swung round with a shrill trumpet, curled up its trunk and charged.

It is said that provided the going is good, and not downhill, an active man can just keep ahead of a charging elephant. Whether this be true I cannot say, but after the first few yards I turned and saw the elephant on the trail about the same distance away, still coming after us. The party had scattered, half coming on with me and the remainder turning back; fortunately no one had a load which hampered running. Then we rounded a bend in the path, and the elephant crashed straight on into the jungle and we saw it no more. Half an hour later stragglers and scattered equipment had been collected, and we continued on our way; but since then I have noticed that my wish to see wild elephants has considerably diminished.

In some areas such encounters with rogue elephants are fairly frequent and during survey operations in the low hills of the Chindwin–Irrawaddi watershed, two wild elephants were killed and another wounded in one season, by surveyors acting purely in self-defence. On one occasion a surveyor and his squad were on a narrow ridge when they encountered and were charged by a wild elephant. The surveyor managed somehow to escape unharmed, but three of his men flung themselves in terror down the steep sides of the ridge, and had to be sent to hospital as the result of their injuries.

It would be a mistake, however, to think that the majority of elephants, or even many of them will attack without provocation. This unpleasant habit is confined practically entirely to rogues, as solitary bulls are called who have been ousted from a herd by some successful rival. A herd of wild elephant will generally make off at the first sign of the approach of man.

Just as vicious, and in some ways more deadly than any rogue elephant, is the hamadryad, or king cobra, fortunately rare in Upper Burma but not uncommon in the eastern foothills of the Arakan Yomas. This snake commonly attains a length of thirteen feet or more, and will attack at sight. Its speed makes any attempt to escape by running, useless. Unlike the elephant, I had no wish whatever to encounter a hamadryad, but it was not long before I did so.

Walking along a narrow jungle trail behind a Burman guide, I suddenly became aware of the largest snake I had ever seen lying beside the path, its head pointed away and its tail not a yard from my feet. The markings on its back and the large hood put its identity at once beyond doubt. It was a very large hamadryad; and the guide had walked right past it within two feet of its head without noticing or disturbing it.

In an instant I had turned about and run back for my shot gun, which was coming along with a coolie a few yards behind. Meanwhile the guide stopped and called out to ask the cause of the delay, and began idly to chop a bamboo with his *dah*. At once the snake was on the alert, and raised its head in readiness to strike. One glance was enough for the guide, who with an exclamation fled. The snake fortunately did not attack but remained with hood erected, and head swaying slightly backwards and forwards, the picture of malignant watchfulness. I rammed a No. 8 cartridge, the first that came to hand, into my gun and hurriedly fired. The range may have been too great for the small shot to be effective, or my aim uncertain, for the snake instead of collapsing, disappeared with a whirl of coils, into the undergrowth down the hillside, and was not seen again.

The seaward slopes of the Arakan Yoma mountains, have a sinister reputation for man eating tigers. Near the crest of the main range there is a small rest-house which must be unique. It is surrounded by a tiger-proof fence. That his protection is necessary, was amply proved by the experience of a party of surveyors who camped a few miles away, one night in January 1929. Four of them were with their camp officer and squads, making a total of about forty men altogether. The surveyors and the officer were sleeping in tents or shelters of bamboo round the edge of the camp, and their *khalasis* and coolies lay on the ground in the centre, surrounded with a circle of fires.

At midnight the camp was awakened by a sudden scream. A tiger had bounded through the circle of fires, seized a sleeping coolie and carried him off. The shouts of the others and the struggles of the man made the tiger drop him, only to pounce on him and knock him down again when he tried to escape. Again the man struggled free, and this time got back to his companions, badly mauled.

The remaining hours of the night were hours of terror. The whole camp stood huddled together behind the circle of dying fires, for which no one dared to fetch more fuel. In the surrounding darkness, the tiger could be heard prowling about, waiting an opportunity to seize another victim; and on one occasion it actually entered a surveyor's tent and pulled about his bedding. With the coming of daylight the tiger went away, and the injured man was hurried down to the nearest hospital, a couple of marches away; but blood poisoning set in and he only survived the journey by a couple of hours.

Nor was this the only victim of the man-eaters of those parts. A few days after the tragedy just related, a couple of Kachin coolies were sent by a surveyor, with a letter, to the camp headquarters at Sandoway. There were no villages for the first two marches, so they had to spend a night in the jungle. This was, however, nothing new to men born and brought up in the frontier hills, and following their usual custom they built a bamboo platform on a tree, seven or eight feet above the ground and went to sleep on it.

Shortly before dawn, a tiger sprang on to the edge of the platform, seized one of the sleepers and pulled him to the ground; where the shouts of the other succeeded in driving it away. At dawn the wounded man took his enamel plate to serve as a basin, and went to a stream a few yards away to wash his wounds.

After some time, as he did not return, his companion called to him, but received no reply. Again he called, but still there was no reply. Now thoroughly alarmed, the man got down from his tree, and ran down the trail, in search of help. After going five miles he met a party of villagers cutting bamboo, and returned with them. Going to the bank of the stream they found the last chapter of the tragedy clearly written in the sand. At the water's edge was the enamel plate and a leather purse, and leading from the spot were the pug marks of a large tiger. No trace of the body was ever found.

In this area, about the same time a European camp officer witnessed a scene which must be rare, if not unique—that of a pair of tigers cooperating in hunting a barking deer. Early one morning, coming quietly over a rise, he caught sight of a tiger a short distance away crouching behind a bush. A moment later, a barking deer pursued by another tiger dashed past the spot. In an instant the first tiger had sprung on it and borne it to the ground. At the same time it saw the officer who had been joined by his men, and both tigers made off, leaving the deer on the ground calling out, but paralysed by a bite in the neck. The men ran forward, despatched the deer and bore it off in triumph, feeling for the first and only time during that anxious period, pleasantly disposed towards the tigers of the Arakan Yomas.

In Upper Burma, tigers, though numerous, are seldom man-eaters; and except for carrying off an occasional mule, cause the surveyor little trouble. Should they take village cattle, the villagers retaliate by setting traps. These are of two types, either cross bows with poisoned arrows, or spring guns, set to go off with a trip wire, or actual traps, working on the principle of a mouse trap, to catch and crush the tiger.

This setting of spring guns once led me into an adventure, which it is pleasant to look back on, but which I would not care to repeat. Survey operations were going on in the southern portion of the Somra Tract, a loosely administered tribal area, in the north-east of the Upper Chindwin district; and I had marched up to Dansagu, a fair sized Kuki village, perched on a hill-top at about 4,000 feet above sea level.

The morning following my arrival, rain and low clouds made work impossible, and I had to remain in my tent. During the morning, news came that a tiger had killed a young mithun, one of the peculiar cattle of the Burma–Assam hills, half bison half domestic cattle; and at the request of the villagers I sat up for it that night. Luck was however against me, for the tiger under cover of the low clouds had returned to the kill during the daytime, and on my arrival, a couple of hours before sunset, there was nothing remaining of it but the head. An extremely uncomfortable wait over this, which voracious blood blister flies made a misery, proved fruitless.

During the next few days work took me elsewhere; but on my return, just before dark one evening, I was told that in my absence the village had been practically besieged by, not one, but a family of tigers. Two more mithun, a couple of pigs and goats had been taken, the last named from right under houses in the village, and the villages were in a great state of alarm. Like all the hill people of the eastern frontier, Kukis are very superstitious, and they attributed their present misfortune to the displeasure of the local *nats*, the spirits who haunt the jungles on the lookout for causes of offence. As the attitude of these people towards the survey had from the first been somewhat uncertain, this state of mind was most undesirable. They might easily decide that our work was the cause of the displeasure of the *nats*, and this would lead to endless complications.

The night before my return a mithun had been killed in a clearing about a thousand feet below the village, and dragged into a patch of very dense jungle, where half of it had been eaten. The villagers had during the day set two ancient flintlock muzzle-loading guns over the remains, with trip wires across the most likely approaches. There was only one muzzle-loader in Dansagu, so the second had been borrowed from a neighbouring village, thus denuding the place of local fire-arms.

At about seven-thirty that night, the stillness was broken by a loud report from the darkness below, followed a few minutes later by another report. Both guns had gone off, but whether monkeys, passing deer or pig, or the tigers had fired them, only the morning would show.

Shortly after daylight the matter was settled. Two individuals accompanied by a crowd of villagers presented themselves at my tent, and informed me that they had been down to the kill to investigate. A tiger had been wounded and was still in the vicinity of the guns, and they had disturbed another tiger a short distance away. One of the men was bleeding from several gashes in his legs and cheek and I thought at first that he had been mauled; but his injuries turned out to have been the result of a fall during a too hasty flight from the vicinity of the wounded tiger.

The villagers asked me to go down and finish off the tiger and enable them to recover their guns. This placed me in a dilemma. To follow one's own wounded tiger on foot through dense jungle is bad enough, but one at least has the feeling of performing a duty; to go after a wounded tiger for which one is in no way responsible is much worse. I had once before had occasion to follow one up and had no wish to repeat the performance. On the other hand the villagers seemed to have such unlimited faith in my shooting powers that I hadn't the face to admit that I was frightened; and in any case it was very desirable to do something towards allaying their superstitious fears about these particular tigers. After some hesitation I decided to go, having first stipulated that I would keep the skin, a proposal to which I thought the villagers agreed almost too readily.

The next move was to the village where we collected half a dozen spears with which I armed the bravest looking men. Then we set off down the trail to the clearing, my two informants acting as guides. After a short way we left the path, and after fifteen minutes were approaching the spot through jungle so thick that it was impossible to see more than five yards ahead. I liked the affairs less and less, but it was now too late to turn back. Then to my relief, light appeared ahead and we found ourselves on the edge of a small ravine running diagonally down the steep hillside.

At the same moment, the silence was broken by a reverberating growl from a thick clump of grass just beyond the ravine. We halted abruptly and assumed the defensive, expecting to be charged; but after half a minute the sound ceased. The growl of a wounded tiger at close quarters is extraordinarily awe inspiring; it is not very loud but it gives the impression of enormous power. We waited a little longer and then crossed the ravine higher up. The tiger was now about forty yards below, on the far side of the patch of grass. In the next few minutes something would happen; we were all keyed up to the highest pitch.

We now formed a compact line, with the spearmen at either side and myself in the centre. Cautiously we moved forwards down the hill, our senses strained to detect the slightest sound or movement from in front. After what seemed hours, but must in reality have been only a few minutes, someone spotted a patch of dull red through the grass—the tiger's shoulder. I quickly put a shot into it, and was answered by a roar before which the line shrank away; then silence once more. Again a cautious advance, and then we came on the tiger lying stretched out at its last gasp.

A final shot finished it off. To my great disappointment it turned out to be not the mother, but a three-quarter grown cub. This, however, made no difference to the villagers, whose return with the dead tiger slung on a pole, resembled a triumphal procession. That evening the event was celebrated with drinking and revelry which were kept up long into the night.

The tigress and the other cub still remained in the vicinity and after a few days, there were further losses of pigs and goats. A fortnight later I was camped once again just outside Dansagu, when the alarming news was received that a raiding party had come over the border from Manipur with the object of securing a couple of heads which the *nats* had demanded. The previous day it had been seen near a village seven or eight miles away, but had since disappeared. The inhabitants of Dansagu were in a state of great alarm, and would not leave their village, except in large parties.

My camp was situated a couple of hundred yards below the village, and at dusk all the villagers turned in and barricaded themselves into their houses. It seemed most improbable that the raiding party would attempt anything in the vicinity of an official known to be armed, so my camp turned in without taking any special precautions. I personally felt sceptical about the story of the headhunters and was soon fast asleep.

About midnight I was awakened by a shout from the next village, about three-quarters of a mile away across the valley. In a few moments it was followed by an uproar. In an instant everyone in the camp was on the alert. Going out of my tent I found the country bathed in moonlight; with the aid of which we could dimly see the village from which the noise was coming. The thought of the headhunters at once leapt to our minds; but the shouting was too far away and confused for us to be able to make out anything definite from it. We called up to the Dansagu people, but they were too alarmed to leave their houses, and refused to come down and discuss the situation.

Presently the shouting died down, and after a further wait, as nothing more occurred we turned in and went to sleep once more; though this time I must confess to some misgivings. In the morning a strong party from Dansagu went to enquire the cause of the disturbance, and found it to have been not headhunters, but the tigress which had come boldly into the village and carried off a young mithun right under the eyes of the villagers. Of the raiding party we heard no more, but I subsequently learnt from a trustworthy source that one really had come over the border after heads, but had thought better of the matter and turned back.

Official duties called me down to the plains in the morning, and that year I had no more news of the tigress. The following year, however, I met the brother of the headman of Dansagu, who came for work as a *khalasi*, and from him I learnt that the tigress had soon afterwards met her fate. She too had fallen a victim to a spring gun.

(1933)

On the Banks of the Narbada

By 'Nimrod'

It is difficult in these days, when the mileage of the working railways in India amounts to 39,049, of which the Indian State Railways control 16,000, to realise the days prior to 1851 when the first section of the Great Indian Peninsula Railway was commenced from Bombay. Then the Narbada river, from the banks of which we write, was accessible only by weeks of travel, much of it through wild and difficult country. Now it is bridged by railways in four places.

The portion of the river where we are is some twenty-five miles north of the G.I.P. Railway, which runs more or less parallel to the river between Khandwa and Jubbulpore.

"Narbada Mai" or Mother Narbada, as it is reverently named by Hindus, is the most sacred of all the rivers of India. It rises to the East of the Central Provinces, on the borders of the State of Rewah, at a place called Amarkantak and enters the sea near the town of Broach after a course of some seven hundred miles.

In former days it formed, with the forests and hills along its course, one of the main barriers which shut off the peoples of northern India from those of the Deccan. At the close of the triumphant career of Samudragupta, the second king of the Gupta dynasty, the Narbada river was his frontier to the South. He did not attempt to retain conquests made south of the river, and returned, about the year AD 330 past the fort of Asirgarh which is seen in these days by railway passengers from the carriage windows as they travel between the junctions of Bhusawal and Khandwa.

The Narbada (Sanskrit Nar-mada "causing delight") is rightly named. It is a beautiful river through most of its course, and to camp on its banks in the cold weather season is truly a delight. In the hotter months of the year the pleasure may be somewhat at a discount, but the sport is more, both as to tiger and panther, and there is the fishing! In the cold weather there is no fishing with rod and line, and water being found in many places away from the river banks, the carnivora are also less easily located.

However, there are always animals in the forests bordering the river, and a ramble along the banks the day after our arrival at camp showed us the old and new tracks of both tiger and panther.

Our camp is pitched in the open, in the vicinity of shady trees beneath which the tents will be placed when the weather gets warmer. Some young buffaloes are procured at an average price of eight rupees, also a couple of goats at about the same rate, and we are ready for shikar. At this season of the year, it is not possible to beat these extensive and dense covers so any slaying of the carnivora has to be done from a machan, of which we have two. One is a full-sized newar (cotton webbing) bed of solid and non-creaky construction, and the other an ordinary dining room chair with the cane removed and newar substituted. This latter can be tied in almost any tree, thus giving a much wider choice as to position.

We make a careful survey of all possible places at which to tie up our baits, and finally decide upon a large shady tamarind tree—some fifty yards from the river bank and alongside a path leading to it—for the big machan. This is about one and a half miles up stream. Less than a mile down stream a shady tree is chosen for the chair, and the place for the poor "boda" to await his blood-thirsty slaughterer is beside a driftwood tree sunk in the sand, a protruding branch affording an excellent hold for the unbreakable rope with which the animal is to be tethered.

There is much-acquired experience in our arrangements. The machan must be well screened all round and from below. Even now, before we are sitting up, some screening is necessary. Nothing should be left to chance. There must be a rest for the rifle and a small peephole, separate from the aperture from which the shot is to be taken so that we can see the "kill" without having to make any movement. Other details include the fixing of nails into the tree trunk, or its branches, on which to hang our waterbottle and any other sundries at convenient places. To the small chair a comfortable rest for the feet is essential, and a small pillow has to be tied where it will allow the head to comfortably rest; for the vigil may be long or it may be short. We have to await the pleasure of our guest to his dinner and we must be in position, especially at this season of the year, by three o'clock in the afternoon.

When all is ready at both the selected places, men are engaged at eight annas a day each—two for each buffalo as they won't go alone—to tie up the baits each evening and visit them each morning about an hour after sunrise. The animals require one's personal attention as to plenty of dry grass to lie upon at night and proper feeding and watering during the day. Also we have two spare animals so as to give each buffalo an alternate "night-in-bed". The moon will be at the full in seven days. This second quarter of the moon is the best—almost the only period—for this "sitting-up", so we hope the tiger or tigress will soon return this way.

Our mind at rest as regards all our arrangements, we take walks abroad to learn our surroundings. We are close to a ferry plying backwards and forwards across the river. The ferry boat is run by a contractor who secures the necessary labour by subsidising the villages on either bank, the people arranging among themselves a "roster of duty". The ferry fees are moderate enough. A loaded cart is two annas, and if with bullocks, three annas. An anna is a consideration, so most of the bullocks have to wade and swim; and there is much shouting and yelling and throwing of stones to make the animals take to the water. A human passenger is taken across for the twelfth part of an anna.

The people of the village on our side are mostly Dhimars—fishermen by caste and occupation but a good deal lower in the social scale than the Bois of the south who are, in most places, hereditary palanquin bearers. It seems likely that as servants—when Europeans first came to India—were largely recruited from the Bhois the term "boy", so much used, is derived from Bhoi. However this may be, these people are clean and industrious at their work of catching fish, which they sell in the surrounding villages at four annas a pound.

There is much life in the river and along its sand banks and islands. We see a crocodile on yonder spit of sand, and nearby, perched on a branch of a submerged tree, is a "snake-bird" as the Indian Darter is called by Europeans and very snake-like he looks when his lean head and neck are protruded from the water. The specimen we see has his wings spread out to dry and looks rather like a church lectern. At a respectful distance from the seemingly sleeping crocodile are two Brahmini ducks—Ruddy Shelldrake to give them their proper name. Wary birds they are, and without good reason, as they are not sought after by European sportsmen and are protected by Hindus, who do not like them being shot. The graceful river terns are seen sweeping easily along over the water, and kingfishers of three varieties are noticed, the black and white kingfisher being less common than the two coloured ones.

Cormorants we also see and that curious bird, the Goggle Eyed Plover, or stone-curlew, is constantly spied as we float silently in our dug-out among the islets of the river. Among the bright green foliage of the dwarf jamun bushes is heard the twittering of many small birds, bulbuls, warblers, sparrows, and the like. A racquet-tailed drongo scolds us as we drift by and we hear the screeching of green parroquets among the trees along the bank. There is the occasional splash of fish, and the wide ripple we see in front of us is caused by a crocodile having slipped silently into the stream.

Indeed the river is a delight, not only on account of the many forms of life we see but on account of the lovely lights and shadows; the waving of the graceful tamarisks and grasses; and the beauty of the sunset which we watch until all the crimson glow has faded away. Then follows the paddling upstream in the moonlight until we arrive at the sandbank just below our camp.

The camp larder is empty and we have to find the wherewithal to fill it, so the morning finds us early abroad with a view to rounding up some of the numerous pea-fowl in the vicinity. This proves an easy matter, and we do not mind firing an occasional shot in the vicinity of camp.

In this way four days pass and then the buffalo downstream is killed by a male tiger. We see by the tracks that he was hunting among the reeds and bushes of the river bed; that he saw the buffalo and rapidly made towards it; that he swam across a small lagoon and then, stealing under the bank in the dark shade of some trees, quickly got within a few yards of his unsuspecting victim, the body of which is now covered with branches weighed down by stones. We have known a branch pulled aside by a prowling jackal to expose a limb to the ubiquitous crow, with the consequent arrival of vultures and the complete destruction of the "kill". We decide that three o'clock will be early enough to be in position, in which we are wrong, as it is while we are completing the screening arrangements that we hear the coughing of langoors announce that the tiger is on the move close by. The men hurriedly unscreen the carcass and make off up the bed of the river.

The suspicions of the tiger have been aroused. He has heard movement at the place; and instead of appearing in daylight as he would probably have done, kept away until 10-30 p.m.

The moon was well above the trees and the kill, in the shadow early in the evening, was now in the light, almost as broad as daylight, of a moon at the full. The stillness of the jungle at night can almost be felt. One could hear a pin drop. So when there is a slight rustle on the bank ten yards away, it is known who has arrived on the scene. After several minutes—we know his attitude of intent listening, watchfulness with all senses on the alert, we hear his heavy approach as he sets aside all caution and comes striding down the steep sandy incline to pass within about twelve feet of the muzzle of the rifle as he goes to the kill. He lifts the carcass with a quick movement, as is almost invariably the case on first arrival, finds it still hard and fast and stands, again listening intently, gazing out over the river bed.

The rifle is raised, sighted, and lowered. There is plenty of time and such preliminary righting shots are a guard against undue haste. It is the first shot that is all important. The stillness of the peaceful night is rent by the tremendous explosion of seventy-five grains of cordite. The tiger lurches to one side, collapses, and slides to the foot of the slope shot through the heart and killed instantly by the terrific impact of the soft nose and split bullet of five hundred grains weight. One moment standing in all his majestic strength and symmetry, the next his life is extinguished, and his death even more merciful than that of the buffalo he slew a few hours before.

To the sound of the signal horn we carry for such occasions, the men come up from the huts half a mile away. The mighty beast is seen, admired and carried up the bank—a difficult business and requiring a number of men as the tiger was nine feet long and weighed three hundred and eighty-four pounds.

The following day is occupied with skinning, and pegging out and curing the skin (for which purpose there is nothing better than burnt alum and saltpetre finely powdered and mixed in the proportion of four parts of alum to one of saltpetre). In doing all this, *experientia docet*, and personal attention to all details ensures a good result. The least one can do before shooting animals is to make sure we know all about the proper preservation of the trophies we seek.

A period of ten days elapsed before the tigress put in an appearance. One of the methods of shooting a tiger is to so arrange an approach to the kill as to enable one to get silently and without discovery within certain shooting distance. Up the river such an arrangement had been made, and for six successive mornings we stalked the tied-up buffalo at dawn, each time in the hope of this, the acme of all tiger-shooting.

On the seventh morning, we wearied of the difficult walking over the stones of the river bed to the sandy path from which the stalk commenced, and took a day off. That very morning the tigress was found to have killed. She was an unwary beast, or very hungry. Having slain the buffalo at about daybreak, as could be known from the tracks along the sand, she appeared in broad daylight, shortly after four o'clock in the afternoon, seized the kill and then stood listening intently and looking up the path along which she no doubt heard the men come when they visited the kill in the morning. She fell in her tracks, instantly slain. Not a move, scarcely a twitch of the tail. And so she came down the river in a dug-out canoe; the beautiful river along the banks of which she had hunted for many years, for she was an old beast. Eight feet two inches she measured and her weight two hundred and forty pounds.

It was to be expected that after these two animals some time would elapse before other tigers took their places, and so it proved. Another year however finds us at the same place: and making similar arrangements we await the pleasure of the tiger and tigress, successors of their departed relatives, who are now in possession.

We are not, alas! to have the same fortune, as the tiger is disposed of by a village shikari over a bullock, some few miles away, and the tigress is the wiliest within our experience.

The tigress killed the upstream buffalo very early one morning and the tracks showed that when she first sighted the tethered animal she stuck out her claws, whisked round, and galloped off to the jungle fifty yards away. She eventually came through the forest and killed. It may be that she would have returned that night to meet her end, but chance in the shape of a village calf she met in the forest intervened, as we learnt next day after a night in the machan, that while we were settling ourselves in she was killing the calf. The carcass could not be found and a second night in the machan was without result.

Another bait was tied up at a new place. This cunning tigress examined it at ten paces but refused to kill. Some days later, stalking along the edge of the reeds about daybreak, she again came on the bait, again turned tail and did not kill. She did not return within our stay and will doubtless be slain in a beat during the hot weather.

So we are tigerless on this occasion, both on account of this cunning beast and because a tiger, swimming across the river, chose to walk downstream instead of up and missed our bait. A traveller, this tiger. We heard the various alarm calls of the jungle folk, soon after sundown, announcing his departure. Tigers take readily to water and often swim the Narbada, even in the cold season.

The pleasure of shikar is not all in successful results. The joy of living the jungle life; the peace, and the being so close to nature, is the greater part of sport. And so, though without trophies on this occasion, we are content, and strike our camp, to proceed to other jungle resorts without any regrets in our minds.

Narbada Mai! We will visit you again!

(1928)

The Haunts of Isabeline

By C.H. Donald

I

It has been a severe winter in the Himalayas, and an early one, but once more the sun shines bright and warm, and green patches of grass here and there, in a great wilderness of dazzling white snow, acknowledge its power and the advent of spring. A flock of lighthearted little choughs circling in the bright blue sky above sing to each other, and convey the joyful tidings to all whom they may concern, that the snow is fast melting from their feeding grounds, and that it is high time to be out and enjoying life in such glorious weather.

Isabeline, the little brown mother bear, hears the call, and pokes her nose out of her hollow at the root of an ancient mountain oak, where she has spent the winter, and given birth to two tiny wee cubs. The nose is followed by a great shaggy head and two little beads of eyes, blinking hard in the glare, roll in their sockets, while her nose wobbles about from side to side, to ascertain from every passing zephyr of the presence of any lurking enemy. Her keen scent, however, tells her that all is well, and that she may leave her two woolly balls and come out. Stealthily a great paw, armed with large white nails, next makes an appearance, and then the whole bear in all her glory of a magnificent winter coat, steps out into the sun, to stretch her weary limbs after her long winter sleep. She can still hear the cry of the choughs far, far above her, as she looks up the valley to the alpine pastures which she knows so well, and slowly she moves off in that direction, her legs so stiff that they have some difficulty in bearing her weight, but at each step they get better, and soon "Isabeline" is well above the forests and revelling in the warm sun.

There is, however, no time for enjoyment and the pangs of hunger must be first attended to, before she hurries back to the little ones in the cave. The sight that meets her eyes on everyside is not very reassuring and there does not seem very much prospect of satisfying her ravenous appetite on these snow-covered slopes, but she sees the little green path and makes for it and is rewarded for her pains by getting a few mouthfulls of luscious young, wild carrot tops, as *hors d'oeuvre*. Thence she slowly makes her way down again, turning over all the big stones she passes and getting from under one, a nest of beetles or ant's larvæ, and under the next a few blades of sprouting grasses, till eventually she finds herself in a ravine, from the side of which all the snow has been blown off by the wind and the grass coming up sweet and green everywhere, and here she makes up for lost time. As she feeds on she becomes aware that she is not the first of her kind that has visited this spot during that morning, and her nose tells her that another has gone over the same ground, only a few hours before her, but there is no time to think of others, as she goes from tuft to tuft, and here and there turns over a stone to see if it conceals anything edible, beneath it.

She is not nearly satisfied, but the sun is high up in the horizon, and it's time that she made her way back to the little ones at home, as it is not safe to wander about at a time when her arch enemy, man, may be about. Day after day she might be seen grazing on the bare plateaux, in the early mornings, and late evenings, and as the snow melts, new pastures come into being, and she has much less difficulty in satisfying her cravings than she formerly had.

Spring has past into summer, and the snow has given place to green fields of grass and flowers of every hue. Masses of dainty primulae, king-cups and anenomes, clothe the plateaux on every side in gay pinks, yellows and purples, whilst a bright patch of blue tells of a bed of little forget-me-nots or gentians, and there on that crag, all by itself, too proud to mix with the rest, waves gently in the breeze, the gem of the mountains, in its wonderful electric blue, the blue mountain poppy.

The little cubs have been all over these hills with their mother, since we last saw her, and though only three months old now, are fine sturdy little specimens, and up to every kind of mischief their ursine brains can devise. In size there is practically no difference between them, and in colour they are identical, except that the one has a small white waist-coat which is almost indistinguishable in the other. In temperament however, they are as the poles apart, and if you could only get near enough to see the wee, restive little beady eyes of each, you could have no doubt as to which had the wits of the family.

I had seen old "Isabeline" on the very first occasion that she had ventured out of her hollow in the tree, and I had from afar, coveted that glossy, light brown winter coat of hers, which I had examined carefully through my glasses, and as she approached the green patch in the snow, she little guessed, poor little lady, how near she was to feeling a rifle bullet smashing through her bones. I, too, had seen the green patch and knew she would go to it, so keeping the spur of the hill between us, had reached a point a few yards above it, just before her, and watched her as she grazed. I had seen that beautiful coat, but I had also seen something else, when she came to within 30 yards of me, which the glasses had not revealed, and which proved her salvation.

This was the lack of hair, in patches, underneath, which showed me that she was the mother of one, if not two little babies which eagerly waited for her arrival, and would starve in their cave if some cruel hand laid her low now. From that date on she became my especial care, and many and many is the time, that I have sat and watched her turning over the boulders and grazing on the grassy slopes, little dreaming how near she was to her enemy, who, for the time being, was also her friend. When "Devil" and "Fool", as I christened the cubs, first made their appearance in public, early in June, I had the good fortune to meet them at very close quarters, without their knowing it, and from that hour fell in love with them, and was determined to have them for my own, but how to get them, without shooting the mother, was another matter altogether. However, there was no hurry and I could afford to wait and watch, and before long got to recognise the one from the other almost as well as the mother could have done. There was something in the Devil's eyes and general saucy devil-may-care look that was quite wanting in poor Fool. It was not only in his eyes but in his general demeanour, for it was not necessary to be near him to be able to recognise him, he was unmistakable 40 yards away.

What it was, I could not tell, but it was there, and if anyone who had never seen the cubs before, had been asked which was

Devil and which Fool he would have pointed them out correctly, the very first shot.

One evening I had gone up for a quiet stroll to Isabeline's haunts; it was a warm afternoon and very still, even at this altitude, and whilst waiting under a rock, I had got drowsy and fallen asleep.

I woke up with a start hearing strange noises somewhere very near, and there to my delight, not ten yards away, embracing each other, were Devil and Fool. Such a time as they were having, on the soft turf, and the mother a few yards below, not taking the least notice of her dear little hopefuls' gambol. This was luck, the wind blew directly from them to me, so there was no possibility of my being winded, and until it changed, or they got above me, I would be able to feast my eyes on their delightful antics. The fond embrace in which I first saw them, culminated in the Fool losing his balance and toppling over with the Devil still holding on to him, and down they went rolling in a ball for a few yards, when Devil loosened his hold, and ran for his mother. Right under her legs he rushed, and then turning round, stood up on his hind legs, with his forepaws on her back, and coyly peeped at Fool from this coign of vantage. I just suppressed a loud laugh, for anything more grotesque than the Devil's rolling eyes and twitching snout, and the poor Fool's tired look and perplexity, would be hard to find. After a couple of seconds or so, Fool too made a rush for his mother's legs, evidently hoping to get a grip of Devil from below, but Devil had played this game before, seemingly, and was prepared, for as soon as Fool emerged on the other side, Devil fell on his back, with both paws firmly gripping Fool's sides and his teeth in Fool's neck, and thus got quite a pleasant little ride at Fool's expense, till his weight brought Fool down on his nose. Up got Devil again, and made for his mother, and Fool, picking himself up, quietly set about following his mother's example and feeding. The Devil, though, was irrepressible, and, not finding Fool sociably inclined, he looked at his mother as much as to say "shall I?" and began tearing up the ground with his forefeet, and backing at the same time, then suddenly made a plunge at her, but evidently rather misjudged his distance, for he landed right on her head, which had the effect of jabbing her snout rather violently into the ground. Next instant old Devil was flying through space as though out of a gun barrel, and landed on his back quite ten feet down the hill. The mother went on with her grazing and took no further interest but the Devil's face was a treat. He stood up and looked at his mother out of the corner of his eye, and such a look!

I am sure that had he been able to speak English, the words he would have muttered would have been "nasty old cat" He could not have expressed himself more plainly than he did, though.

Now this would probably have kept Devil quiet for some time, and made him think of more serious things, but just then he looked up and his eye met Fool's, in which he plainly saw written the words "that served you jolly well right", and that coming from Fool was not to be endured at any price, so he made a savage charge at him, and once again I saw them in a loving embrace, but this time they had both got a good deal to say to each other as they rolled down, locked in each other's arms, and from the way it was all said, I knew it was nasty names that they were calling each other. A depression in the ground hid them from my view for a few seconds, and what was my surprise to suddenly hear the angry "unf unf unf" half sneeze, half grunt of a bear alarmed, and angry. Up went the mother's head in a second, with her nose held well to the wind, and giving vent to a deeper "unf unf unf" than the last I had heard, off she went, after Devil and Fool, but pulled up at the top of the depression, where I could still see her, with all the long hair on her withers bristling with anger, at something I could not see. The babies had both now joined their mother and all there stood looking down at, to me, the unknown disturber of their peace.

What could it be? Not a man, for they would not stand there looking at him, and besides, there were no shepherds on this plateau as yet, and nobody but a shepherd would come here. I began to get as excited as the bears were, but could not move from my rock without attracting the attention of one or the other of the three before me, so had to curb my impatience and sit where I was, but was soon rewarded, for the mother gradually edged off and down into the depression and both the cubs followed. I was out of my hiding at once, and taking advantage of a small spur behind one got quickly round it.

As my head got over the rising ground, the breeze brought up the shrill "chick chick" constantly repeated notes of the monaul pheasant, this also was his note of alarm and warning, but far down in the valley.

With my glasses I searched every inch of the rolling plateaux before me and below me, but not a thing could I see anywhere, and yet I felt certain that something was astir somewhere, what could it be?

Just as I was getting tired of looking at nothing, a movement a long way down the hill caught my eye, but look as I would nothing could I make of it, though I gazed again and again with a powerful pair of Zeiss glasses, at the exact spot where I had seen the movement with the naked eye. Looking still lower down, I suddenly spotted a fox digging for voles some 200 yards below where I had first seen the "movement."

This would account for the cry of alarm of the monaul, but did not in the least explain the uneasiness of the bears, or that "movement" I saw. Still worried, I kept on looking at the fox, a tiny speck in the distance, when again that movement caught my eye, and much more distinct this time. Again I got the glasses out and looked and looked till my eyes ached, but nothing was visible, and yet I was sure that I was not mistaken. More puzzled than ever, I decided to watch the country around the fox for a few minutes, and before a couple of minutes had gone I distinctly saw a greyish object flash through the air and again disappear into the very bowels of the earth. Again my glasses revealed nothing, for some time, but at length, on a grey boulder, I noticed the twitch of a tail, and there right before me, was a beautiful panther crouching low on the rock. I must have had my eyes and glasses on him over and over again, and yet not seen him, and now that I had seen him, he was as plain almost as the bears had been a few minutes previously. It was absurd to risk a 400 yards long shot, but how was I to get nearer in such open country, was the question? But then again why those sudden movements on his part and why was he now crouching on that rock?

Then a thought struck me. He was stalking the fox. If so, that would be something worth watching, and I soon forgot all about Isabeline and her family and settled myself to watch developments in this direction, For five full minutes that panther sat immovable as the rock on which he crouched, and then without a moment's warning or the slightest movement of a muscle, he sprang straight into the air and stopped dead on a rock some ten feet lower down, in the identical position in which he left the last rock. I looked at the fox but she had noticed nothing, and was moving leisurely about in quest of her voles. The next move of the panther was different, and he sprang lightly off the rock and crouching low, went very stealthily yet with quick steps, down the hill. This time the fox looked up, and immediately the panther crouched and lay still. The fox, however, like me, had got a glimpse of something and though not scared, was still suspicious and kept looking up every few seconds, but the panther never moved a muscle, and only about 80 to 100 yards divided them.

Gazing through binoculars for any length of time is very tiring for the eyes, and though loth to miss a single state of the drama before me, I put them down till the feline should again make a move, keeping my eyes on him in the meantime. It was about 10 minutes ere he moved again and this time covered a good 20 paces ere he stopped, but the fox too was changing her ground and still kept her distance. She was now no longer straight below him as she had been when I first saw him, but had got several yards to one side, yet he still went on straight down.

Could he have lost sight of her, and is he making for the place he last saw her in, from the rock, in the fond hope that she is still there? Not much fear of his taking those all-seeing eyes of his off her for a single second. I soon saw his little game; there was a huge rock some 30 feet to the rear of the fox and he meant to get that between him and her as soon as possible. A slight pause of a few seconds and as the fox did not look up, he moved stealthily forward and got on to a rock and very slowly peered over. The little fox still merrily went from hole to hole, noising each, oblivious of all danger, and as she turned her back for a second, I saw a sight I shall never forget.

The panther had been looking over the rock at the time, with his fore paws resting on it and his hind feet on the ground below, and yet from that non-jumping attitude, he sprang clear 20 feet or so down, and looked for all the world like a shooting star. This spring and a rush and he was behind the coveted rock, but what in the meantime had alarmed the fox? She was not looking in his direction, but rather down the hill and below him, yet "pheaw pheaw-aw-aw" came her long warning cry.

I could no longer see the panther now, but knew he was only waiting for the fox to turn her head, and she was as good as dead, and then, perhaps I might have a chance of a stalk after him. The fox looks this way and that, undoubtedly alarmed, but unaware of the cause of it. Some wonderful instinct warning her to be on her guard, for what else could it be that alarmed her? Had it been some sound the feline made, or had she got his scent, she would have run off some distance away from either, before turning to "pheaw," but it is something in no way located, yet she is aware in some vague way of the presence of danger.

It comes too; as she turns her head there is a mighty rush, and a something with the speed of a falcon is on her, almost before she has time to look back, but there again, that something has befriended her, and with a sudden whisk of her tail, and a twist that my eye could not even follow, she has evaded those relentless talons, and somehow doubled under the panther's legs and is flying for life down the hill, to find cover in the birch jungle below. Strangely enough the panther never even attempted to follow, but accepted his defeat, and sat down on a rock and watched the fox racing down the hill. I could hear the "pheaws" coming up from the forest below, for a long time after.

I carefully changed my position and getting into a dip of the hill crawled round till I got a ridge in between myself and the feline, and then ran as hard as I could for a spot I marked out in my mind as being within 100 yards of him, and arriving there, stalked very carefully over, till I could get my eyes just over the top, but he was "non est".

High and low I searched, but not a sign of him could I find and as night was fast approaching, I had to make my way back to camp, and leave him.

II

In the meantime, while I interested myself in the panther and his doings, Isabeline and her cubs had wandered out of sight, and I saw them no more for some time to come. I had rather wondered at the bears giving their note of alarm for a panther, and I do not suppose that a solitary one would have bothered his head much about him one way or the other, but with a mother with tiny cubs, it is different, as Mr Spots would not hesitate long about making a meal off a cub if he got the chance, and Isabeline had long ago taught Devil and Food to be careful of his scent, and warn her at once should they come across it.

I have already said that I had wanted to capture the cubs and have them as pets, but one cannot go and shoot an animal one has taken an interest in for over a month, in cold blood, though I have no doubt, had I seen her with the cubs the first time she came out, I should not have thought twice about it. The next time I came across them, the summer had given place to late autumn, the sheep had left the alpine pastures, the flowers had bowed their heads to the cutting winds, and the glorious verdant carpets on which Devil and Fool had been wont to play had assumed a sombre brown. In the valley below, the birch and maples had clothed themselves in their golden tints, and lower still could be seen the brilliant scarlet of the virginian creeper clustering about the dark green of the spruce and silver-fir.

The scene in all its wonderful variety of colours, even though it lacked the vivid greens of spring, defied description. Above, the grand old giants reared their virgin snow-capped peaks into the clear blue sky, and in the gorge, just below that mighty peak, a glacier grim, glistened with blues and greens as the rays of the morning sun touched it.

Well might Isabeline be proud of her lovely haunts, and loth to leave them till the bleak winter winds and hard frosts which made digging impossible, drove her down to more sheltered nooks. The hardy "bhurrel", the blue sheep of the Himalayas can alone face those icy blasts, and appears to revel in the blizzards that howl round his inhospitable, rugged peaks.

As soon as the frost sets in, and even Isabeline's great claws and forearm can make no impression on the hard ground, she thinks of looking about for a sequestered home in which to spend the winter. A cave beneath an overhanging rock, or the hollow at the root of a tree, which will keep her warm and dry and yet permit the passage of fresh air, are selected with much care, for her long winter sleep. She will enter it a fat tubby ball, almost round, and issue four to five months later, simply skin and bone, but the possessor of a lovely coat.

It was in late October, when I came across Isabeline and her cubs. The latter were now well grown, and to catch them would have been no easy matter, so I was obliged to give up all thought of it, but my interest in them had not abated in the slightest and I was as ready as ever to watch them at their play. Determined to find out their hibernating quarters, I used to be up on their feeding grounds before the sun touched them and on the first occasion contented myself by watching them leave for the trees, as the day advanced, through my glasses. But that proved a fruitless watch, as I lost sight of them as soon as they got into the forest.

The next time, some ten days later, I decided to follow them, but the ground being caked and hard with frost, I had the greatest difficulty in seeing their tracks, and lost them entirely in the forest, where they went over a succession of rocks and boulders. The following week a light fall of snow came to my help, and the morning after it, I made my way up to her favourite ravine and was just in time to see her and the cubs disappearing into some birch jungle. There was no mistaking their tracks now, and on hands and knees I crawled after them among the dense tangle of branches which being bent down year after year by the winter snows, grow down instead of standing up straight.

Careful not to get too near or disturb them in any way, I carefully avoided each branch, either stepping over or crawling under it. Thus I must have covered over a mile, and was thankful to find myself getting into more open cover, the birch giving place to oak and pine. All this time I had not got a single glimpse of them, though I know from the tracks that I was very near. Under one tree I found marks of the mother's claws, where she had raked up some twigs and branches, preparatory to lying down for the day, but had changed her mind and moved on. This at all events meant that she would not go very much further and it behoved me to be all the more careful, in case I stumbled on to her unawares from below, in which case she might charge and tend to make things nasty, in defence of her cubs.

I had my trusty rifle with me, but there are times when it is difficult to be quick enough with it, and this might be one of them. Carefully, with one eye on the tracks and the other on the ground ahead, I plodded on, removing every twig that chanced in my way, and to my joy I at last came to where the tracks began moving downhill. This gave me a much better command of the position and also enabled me to see further. A bear, brown or black, if he selects a tree to sit behind, will almost invariably sit on the upper side and not below it, so I should now have a chance of seeing the family from some distance if they meant to sleep under a tree and not go into a cave, which at this season, however, was unlikely.

On the other hand, this would not help me to find, their hibernating quarters, but having come so far, I intended to continue now, wherever they went, and follow them. A tragopan gave me the first intimation of their exact whereabouts, for not 50 yards ahead, I could hear his plaintive cry as, disturbed by their approach, he rushed up the hill uttering his curious single note. This meant that I could hurry on for a few paces, as a spur divided us, and any noise I made would not reach them, but I must be careful not to frighten the tragopan unduly and make him fly, as that might put the bears on the *qui vive*.

The bears had not wasted their time while seeking their place for the mid-day siesta, as over-turned stones and logs of wood testified, and in one place I had to make a dive into some undergrowth to avoid a nest of angry jungle wasps, whose home had been ruthlessly torn out and their winter store of honey robbed by the furry marauders ahead.

A musk-deer near whose lair they passed, stood up and gave his cry of alarm—"fitch fitch"—at intervals of a few seconds, and so engaged was he in looking at the bears, that I got to within 30 feet of him, and could see his gleaming white tushes and saw him stamp his foot, as he "fitched" and wagged his little scut.

One ear was held forward and the other twitching back and fro, alive to every sound. I crouched behind a stump and very gently "fitched" in return. In a second his head turned in my direction, and he stood staring intently, not being able to make it out, the very embodiment of grace and daintiness. I dare not alarm him or he might go racing off down the hill in his succession of jumps, a mode of locomotion, peculiar to the little beasts, and yet I must get him away from here, before I could move myself, and in the meantime, the bears were getting further and further away. "Fitch fitch" I said to him and "fitch sh sh" was his reply, and a violent stamp on the ground. A second "fitch" from me was too much for his nerves and had the desired effect. With half a dozen dainty little bounds, all four legs rising and falling at the same time, he fled up the hill and with a final "fitch" disappeared from view behind some rocks.

Again I moved forward and, climbing a small rise over which the tracks led me, looked down on an expanse of melting snow and at the foot of it saw Devil and Fool playing hide and seek. Glancing at the tracks, I could see that they had not troubled to walk down, but had simply glissaded or rolled the whole way to the bottom. Even Isabeline had become playful after her slide, for, as one of the cubs ran round her, she got up on her hind legs, her great fat forearms swaying from side to side, and gave vent to a loud snort ending up with a tremendous puff as though blowing bubbles.

Little Fool rushed up and also got on to his hind legs in front of her, and the pair promptly set to work to do a little boxing, but Devil did not see why he should be left out in the cold, and made for poor Fool. A fair spar, with the mother as umpire, ensued, but as usual it did not last long and ended up in close grips and a roll in the snow. Devil's honour was satisfied and once more the trio started off up the opposite hill, and I had to sit where I was till they went round the next spur, and once more took up the trail from the next ridge.

I had been most fortunate all this time in having the wind blowing down hill, but it was now time for it to change. In the Himalayas the wind usually blows down the valleys from 4 or 5 o'clock in the afternoon till 8 or 9 a.m. the following morning, and uphill for the rest of the day, but this fact would not trouble me so long as the bears kept to the contour of the hills, but if they suddenly went down a valley I should be discovered at once if I attempted to follow, so in that case I would have to wait till they had climbed up the other side.

As I topped the crest I found before me a ravine covered with a forest of spruce and silver-fir, and now left convinced that this was the place the bears had been making for, and would now lie up under some old forest giant. Nor was I wrong. Just below me was the tree they had selected for their seista the previous day, but now they had gone down lower, and I must be cautious as they might come to a halt any moment. I crawled along a few paces and was pulled up sort by hearing a twig crack, and peeping round the trunk of a tree, I espied Isabeline busy making up a snug bed for herself, and both the cubs interestedly watching operations.

Foiled in my hopes of seeing their winter quarters I took my sandwiches out of my pocket and proceeded to replenish the inner man, and at the same time keep an eye on the bears. Having removed any stones or hard twigs from under her, the old lady sat up on her haunches and had a good look all round, with her nose well to the wind. Satisfied that all was well she thought about attending to her toilet. A great big hind paw began very deliberately scratching the back of her head and, that done, she lay down with both her fore-paws in front of her and surveyed her huge white claws. Devil still had something on his mind and went down a little way to investigate the roots of another tree, but Fool sat down alongside his mother and getting his hind foot into his mouth, was busy for the next ten minutes sucking it, making an extraordinary gurgling the while. Devil too came up and joined the other two, and half an hour from the time they arrived there everyone was sound asleep, bunched close together. Even though I had seen them settle themselves, I could not make out where one began or the other ended. They looked like one great brown stone except for the fact that every now and again a puff of wind stirred the hair on one of their backs. There was nothing now left for me to do, but to get back home, but before doing so, I would give them a chance of winding me, to see if they kept their noses open even in sleep.

Going back over the spur I had just come over, I descended to their level and quietly got some 20 yards below their tree and hid myself behind another. I had not been there many seconds, when a small head looked round the edge, the nose well in the air and working vigorously, and with a low "unf unf unf" awoke the other two. Both the cubs took to their heels up the hill but the mother waited just long enough to see that nothing followed, and then went after her sons. Their education had not been neglected, evidently, and the mother no doubt was not a little proud of her apt pupils. Had I not seen them go off I might have passed them within a few yards and never known that there was a bear within a mile of me, so quietly had they all disappeared. Fortunately for mother bear, in the Higher Himalayas there is so very little that can harm her of her young that she can instruct them pretty thoroughly as to what they should avoid.

"All man's scents are not necessarily dangerous but it is as well to steer clear of them all. That which is tainted with the smell of goat and sheep, or with that of cows and buffaloes, you need not run from, but just get out of his way and get behind a log or a tree till he has passed. If it is pure man's scent, whether he means mischief or not, fly the moment you get it, and keep to thick scrub as long as you can till well out of his reach, and then go over all the stones and rocks you can find to leave no track. If you get the smell of a panther, give me warning, and keep near me. Goats and sheep are very nice eating but do not go too near a flock while it is still light, unless you can find a straggler. Beware of a flock with which there is smell of dog, as they will bark and rouse the camp and guide the men on your scent, and you will have to give up your dinner even if you have had the luck to get it away. You will be a match for any two or three dogs, but you can do nothing when the dogs are followed by half a dozen men armed with big sticks. Buffaloes will do you no harm if you do them none, and though our cousin the black bear has no difficulty in killing them now and again, and we are stronger than he, yet he has got sharp claws with which he can get a firm hold on the back of a buffalo and so hang on till the animal becomes frantic, and falls over a cliff or breaks a leg, but our claws are no good for that sort of thing, being meant only for digging. The same applies to cows and bullocks, though when you are full grown you may be able to manage a cow, but be careful, as sometimes one or two of the bulls with the herd may charge, and in the open, he will get the best of it. A wheat crop is a very pleasant place to spend a night in, but if grazing is good in our own haunts eschew such luxuries, as they are often fraught with danger, and if it is known that we make raids on the crops, a man with a gun may be there in hiding to receive you one night. Keep to your own lovely feeding grounds, and follow the instructions I have so often drummed into your heads and you will live to be as old as you desire, but remember that curiosity killed the cat, and will be the end of you, if you are not very careful."

The advice was good, and though curiosity was Devil's besetting sin, he was getting over it as he grew up, and after the one or two frights his mother gave him, began to learn that it was enough for him to discover the presence of danger through his nose, without trying to see it as well.

Eighteen months went by, and I had not been able to visit the haunts of Isabeline again, but I had heard of her and the cubs, now grown almost as big as herself, from shepherds and others who had spent the preceding summer near her. Three bears always together, had been frequently reported to me, but no one had ever feared of them attacking sheep, but of late, one huge beast had also taken up his quarters and he had done a good deal of damage among the flocks.

The villagers had begged me to go up and shoot him, and one old man who had been with me on two or three occasions when I had followed up Isabeline and had thought me crazy for not having shot her instead of going miles and miles for the sake of "looking" at her, was careful to inform me that it was not the mother with cubs that the villagers referred to.

It was June ere I got a chance of paying the dear old haunts a visit. Devil and Fool would now be 28 months old and well able to look after themselves. Would I still be able to tell one from the other and when I did see them, would I forget all past associations and shoot on sight, or would I be as eager to watch their antics as of yore?

The second day after arriving on the scene, two bears were seen on a plateau some distance from camp, but too late in the evening to permit of my making a closer acquaintance on that day. Next morning I left camp before it was light and found myself far up on the highlands ere the first streaks of dawn touched the peaks ahead, and shortly after, my glasses revealed one solitary bear, and, if size was any criterion, the veteran who had done the damage among the flocks. Half an hour's careful stalking brought me to within a few yards of where I had last seen him and a cautious look round showed him sitting on a patch of snow, meditating over his many misdeeds.

A low whistle roused him and he cocked his ears and peered round in the direction of the sound, but did not move his position. A depression in the ground served me admirably to run round and get in front of him, but he had heard me moving and was now on the alert though still sitting where I had left him. A snap shot was the work of a moment, and the monster's life blood dyed the white snow beneath him a bright crimson.

Later on I found Isabeline—alone. Devil and Fool had been driven from her side by the big beast whose hide now covers the floor, and the little mother roams the alpine pastures still, and has long forgotten the existence of her young hopefuls.